THE
MI5 GIRL
IN
OXFORD

THE
MI5 GIRL IN
OXFORD

SOPHIE DOLL

BROWN
DOG
BOOKS

Published under licence by Brown Dog Books and
The Self-Publishing Partnership Ltd, 10b Greenway Farm, Bath Rd,
Wick, nr. Bath BS30 5RL, UK

www.selfpublishingpartnership.co.uk
www.themi5girlinoxford.com

ISBN printed book: 978-1-83952-912-2
ISBN e-book: 978-1-83952-913-9

Cover design by Kevin Rylands

Printed and bound in the UK

This book is printed on FSC® certified paper

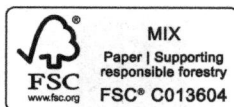

MIX
Paper | Supporting
responsible forestry
FSC® C013604

The secret of happiness is freedom and the secret of freedom is courage.

Thucydides.

DISCLAIMER.

All episodes in which university authorities or police officers bow and scrape to our current in-vogue Orwellian idols are either fictitious or have been relocated from elsewhere.

PROLOGUE

'Megan, is there anything I can offer this guy with his coffee?'

'Er ... there's a fruit cake here in a bag.'

'Sorry? Why are you in a bag?'

'Ho, ho. Aren't we funny?' My sister hammered me none too lightly on the head, picked up her sports kit and left for a game of squash.

The door-bell rang of this, our parents' old pre-fab in Harlech.

'Matthew Sleight?'

'Yes ... and Sophie Hughes?'

'Come in. Roderick said to expect you.'

An academic in his fifties, he had a gentle though husky voice and a tic whereby his head twitched sideways at intervals.

'Sit down, please.'

He did so. 'Sophie, I understand you've finished your degree and are looking for a job?'

'Yes, unfortunately.'

'How about Oxford?'

'There are worse places, I daresay?'

'Yes. Rome under Nero springs to mind ... or Russia?'

I gave a puzzled look.

'My niece, Imogen, is having a tough time there.'

'Oh?'

'She's just finished her first year. She's reading fine art and Biblical Hebrew at Newlove College ... '

'So joint honours?'

'Yes.' He bit his lip.

I started to make the coffee and to cut up the fruit cake on the old wooden dresser.

'She faces two threats. One, a bunch of spiteful student activists who enjoy hurting her ... '

'Fruit cake?'

'Yes please,' he said softly.

I peered over my shoulder. 'Are these bullies identifiable?'

'She can name some of them.'

'Doesn't the University have to act?'

'Spineless academics, incognito bureaucrats ... plus bigotry, cowardice ... what happens? Nothing.'

I placed our coffee cups and cake-plates on the kitchen table and sat down again. 'So how would I fit in?'

'I'm a fellow of Exeter College, but am also writing a monograph titled, *The Newcastle and North Shields Railway*. If you were my research assistant, you would have access to the University's libraries, computers, sports facilities ... '

'I know nothing about railways.'

He gave a wry smile. 'You're very straight.'

I gave a small shrug.

'Roderick is an old school friend and – as you perhaps know – works in intelligence. I asked him if I should employ a private detective, but he doubted that he would get very far. With university membership, he thought you might be able to rub shoulders with ... or even deflect ... these adversaries.'

'Is Imogen a bit of a loner?'

'Yes ... but not unhappily so.'

'Hmm.'

'This cake's good.'

'Supermarket special. What do her parents say?'

'Her mother ran away eleven years ago, I believe to Canada and her father – my brother – lives in France.'

I bit into my cake. 'In what way do these students harm her?'

'Spill drink on her laptop, throw eggs at her, steal her cardigan, taunt her, send the police round because the tiny gold cross she wears round her throat has offended some Moslem. Her tutor is very good, but he himself is in a precarious position with some inquiry hanging over him.'

I poured more coffee. 'How deeply is she affected?'

'She's stoical, resilient. She just takes it ... but it's unfair ... it's wicked.' A few long stray hairs stuck out from his otherwise thin eyebrows, hinting at madness.

I nodded slowly.

'The second strand is a touch more cryptic. Some staff members wish – covertly – to expel her.'

'Why?' I winced.

'She won a scholarship ... and she's extraordinarily talented.'

'So ... what don't they like?'

'Basically it seems, that she's far more gifted than any of them.'

I sucked in my cheeks. 'You don't sound too enchanted with Oxford?'

'I tell you, it's like the Stasi.' He exhaled slowly. 'If you speak the truth – as with Cassandra – everyone is either deaf or they rebuff you.'

'She prophesied that the wooden horse would bring ruin to Troy?'

'Yes.' He sipped his coffee. 'Imogen's professor is very kind, but he floats around on a cloud ... and some of his subordinates are just vile.'

I stared at Matthew. 'But how could I influence any of this?'

'They sent someone to break into her flat, but an anonymous but principled insider jotted down the plot and posted it to Imogen.'

'So you have a lead?'

'The caller rang the buzzer for a top-floor flat, said he had a parcel for Imogen and would she let him pop it through the outer door? I had hidden myself in the lobby. I tip-toed up behind the intruder and photographed him trying to pick her lock. He tried to seize my phone, but Imogen – who came out of her darkened flat – took it and hid it.'

'What did he intend to do?'

'We don't know.'

'Could you identify him?'

'No. Thin, six-foot, white ... but the light was poor and the picture's a rear-view.'

'Goodness.'

'On the basis of the note and the subsequent photograph which tallied, Imogen launched a grievance ... '

'Go on.'

'A reply came from an exorbitantly expensive barrister ... '

'Do lowly sub-orbitally expensive ones exist?'

'Three thousand pounds he charges, to send a letter.'

'A touch on the high side?'

'Its sub-text was that Imogen should tread warily, since

criticisms against her were also under review.'

'A subtly camouflaged threat for her to infer?'

Matthew scraped together his cake crumbs and took a deep breath. 'Will you give it a go?'

The task was hard to picture, yet I quite like a bit of intrigue. I eyed him gravely, then smiled. 'Yes.'

He smiled too, perhaps with a tinge of relief.

We clinked our coffee cups.

'What are you doing at present?'

'I've a summer job in Porthmadog, in a shop which sells pointless junk to tourists; tea-towels printed with unfunny jokes or off-cuts of metal screwed together to make frogs. The only real joke is the sign, "For discerning customers". It's comic nirvana.'

I offered him more cake and he chose the lump with three cherries in it.

'This barrister, Mervyn Grieff Q.C., is acting – I discovered – for the prosecution at the trial of a former soldier accused of shooting dead an I.R.A. gun-man, back in 1988. So on Monday, I went and sat in the public gallery at the Crown Court in Oxford, to watch him perform.'

I emptied my coffee cup.

'The soldier was taken through the events by his own lawyer in a straightforward way. Grieff then stood up and wagging a finger, said, "You said," and quoted back something the soldier had said but with one word changed. He then tied the poor fellow in knots.'

'My dad was in the army. I don't know how these bastards sleep at night?'

'After the session ended, I went to the cafeteria and by chance sat at the next table to this smarty-boots.'

'Oh.'

'A sallow-hued lass brought him a small envelope sealed with red wax.'

'And?'

'Grieff opened it, took a note from it, photographed it with his phone and then tore it into tiny pieces before throwing it and the envelope into a bin.'

'More coffee?' Matthew declined.

'When everyone had gone, I took the plastic bag with its contents out of the bin and stuffed it into my bag.'

'A bold move.'

'The envelope just had his name scrawled on it, "Mervyn Grieff".'

'Handwritten?'

'Yes. When I fitted the note's thirty-two bits together ... ' He brought up a photo on his phone.

It began, 'Midday, Saturday the 4th. of July, 2020.'

'Three days hence,' I observed.

Then came, 'Clue: ? culvert.'

'The plot thickens,' I added.

Its third and last line read, 'NT' followed by eight numbers, two blocks of four.

'A grid reference?'

'That was my thought, but it's in some barren valley in northern Northumberland ... close to the Scottish border.'

'Is eight digits quite exact?'

'It's a ten-metre by ten-metre square.'

'Do you want me to go there?'

'No. I've no idea what it's about. It won't be linked to Imogen ... and it could be dangerous ... or we could just be barking up the wrong tree?'

'It's curious though.'

He finished his second piece of cake. 'I have a second cousin, Lucinda, who has a small flat in the attic of her house in Canterbury Road, which she is willing to let to you. She knows vaguely of Imogen's troubles, but should only know of you as "my research assistant".'

'This all seems a bit hush-hush?'

'I know, but I'm really not sure who to trust.'

We shook hands, he left and I put a pizza in the oven.

A sweat-bedewed Megan came in and flopped into a chair.

As I handed her a glass of juice and some pizza, she said, 'I bumped into Lucy Chalk. They've given you a *rôle* in that play at the castle.'

I was over the moon. I love amateur dramatics. I almost danced a jig.

'Only a small part though, so more of a crumb than a roll.'

I stuck my tongue out. We do not bother with looking 'mature' when alone.

'So what did this mystery guy want?'

'He's given me a job.'

'Oh, good. So for once it didn't end up like a sketch for a *Pink Panther* sequel? Doing what?'

'Um ... '

'Stocking shelves? Ruling the world?'

'Well, he offered the latter, but it sounded too much like hard work.'

Megan gave a frustrated sigh. 'Come on.'

'Ancient rulers often sought conquests because they wanted immortality,' I babbled, 'to become gods ... Caesar at least has a salad named after him, but ... '

'What's the frigging job?'

'Yes, Megan *fach*. Being a guardian angel to a persecuted student ... sort of?'

Megan knitted her brows.

'Yes ... it's a trifle obscure.'

'Clearly then a task for Inspector Clouseau to unobfuscate?'

'"Unobfuscate"? Where did that ridiculous word come from?'

'It sounds good though?'

'It almost *does* obfuscate ... and so contradict itself.' I changed topics. 'Was Romeo at the gym?'

Megan grinned slyly. 'Yes. He's not exactly god-like though, is he?'

'Without a god, then by extension human love cannot transcend the mortal,' I teased.

Megan growled softly, 'Do we want it to transcend the mortal?'

CHAPTER ONE

Dad's old Land Rover is mechanically sound but it rattles a lot. He thought there might be a lump of rubber missing from a tyre, but could not see anything.

Anyway, it is sturdy if utilitarian and I quite like it.

I studied a map of the Cheviots and pin-pointed Borehow Burn amid the thinly settled moors close to the Scottish Borders.

The grid reference was three hundred yards east of an overhead power-line, as indicated by a thin straight line with little inward-facing arrow-heads touching it. From orienteering competitions, I remembered them being reliable guides, unlike Forestry Commission plantations which had always been chopped down and replanted somewhere else since the map you were holding had been drawn.

I drove up on the Friday and just before the town of Wooler, found the turn. I passed between the stone abutments of a former bridge on a dismantled railway line, splashed through a ford and rattled over a cattle-grid before the lanes grew narrower and the gently undulating terrain, more bare.

The grid reference fixed on a derelict and roofless shepherd's hut of which only the crumbling stone walls remained.

In this shallow valley, bounded by low overlapping hills sprinkled with clumps of yellow gorse, brown heather and an occasional scree of grey rocks, the burn bubbled along in its boulder-strewn course.

I spent the night at The Hog's Head Inn outside Alnwick.

The next morning I took a left fork a mile before the shepherd's hut, with the intention of observing it from a hillock a little to its south.

Beyond Scorestone Farm the grey short-wheelbase Land Rover bumped along this twisty track, until – after one mile – I stopped at a five-bar gate. If I crossed this meadow, hid my vehicle behind that copse and walked towards the broad parallel valley, I should be well placed to watch the hut.

I hopped out, opened the gate, drove into the field, then closed the gate.

Suddenly a huge black bull appeared. It circled the Land Rover, snorted a few times and looked decidedly aggressive.

Inside the vehicle I was safe enough, but this crazy myopic animal would not go away.

'What's the matter?' I met its eye. 'I'm not trying to mount a cow.'

It raised its head and gave a deep reverberating moo.

The ground was dry, so I drove round the field trying to shake it off and eventually put enough distance between myself and it to nip out, open the second gate, drive out quickly and shut it before it caught up. I clutched the top of the gate. 'Bye-bye.'

'Mooooo.'

I waded through a swathe of bracken to a knoll of tufty grass, where I settled myself down to await events.

I wore a pair of ex-marine combat trousers, walking-boots, thick socks and a short cagoule.

I opened my rucksack, took out a flask of tea and a

cheese bun and tried to read a book about early railways.

An hour went by. Eleven-thirty. Still no sign of anything. Then as I lowered my old Barr and Stroud ex-army binoculars, I saw a wiry vicious-looking coloured fellow striding towards me.

'What are you doing, prowling around here?'

Since I could think of no sensible excuse, I scrambled to my feet and tried to make a run for it, but he cut off my retreat and grabbed the front of my cagoule. 'Who the hell are you?'

Five years before I had attended a self-defence course, yet had never kept any of it up. His loose jacket though reminded me of a judo throw, in fact the only manoeuvre I still recall.

I grabbed his left sleeve at the elbow with my right hand and his right collar with my left, whilst hooking my left leg behind his legs and trying to throw him forcefully to my right. If done quickly and so catching the opponent off guard, they should lose their balance.

It almost worked ... but not quite.

He then gave me a good punch in the face.

I ran with him in pursuit. I saw the tumble-down remains of an old barn and an abandoned rusty harrow near the copse.

Gasping desperate prayers, I tried to run round them, but he caught me and tried to force me down into the long grass. This time though, it was I who held my ground. I pushed back with all my might and as the shafts of the harrow were close behind his calves, unable to step back, he toppled over backwards.

It took me some time to realise what had happened, but

his head had hit some sharp corroded iron spike and it had punctured his skull.

He started to fit uncontrollably.

On my homeward journey I spotted a skip in a lay-by, threw my old hiking-boots into it and drove on in only my thick socks.

Back in Harlech, Megan examined my black eye.

'How did *that* happen?'

'Don't ask.'

As we ate minestrone soup she said, 'Sophie, do you not think you should ditch this Oxford lark?'

'No,' I replied firmly. 'I'm sticking with it.'

She nodded resignedly. 'I knew you would say that.' She almost burst into tears.

*   *   *   *

A week later I made my last sale in the gift shop; a black china dog with a yellow china butterfly perched on its nose.

'Oh isn't he sweet?' cooed the woman. 'Be careful when you pack him up.'

I dread to think what my face looked like.

Our parents were still away in Cyprus.

Uncle Hywel called. He is a local Methodist preacher. 'I'm changing my car. The part exchange figure for the old Polo is less than the discount if there is no part exchange. Fifty quid?'

'Oh yes!'

'She's reliable, but rattles a bit.'

'I'm used to bone-shakers.' I gave him a big hug and he blew his nose on a large red handkerchief.

Megan tried again to make me give up Oxford. 'What *you* need is a boyfriend.'

I sighed. 'That's true, but I can't force it.'

'That fixed *Mona Lisa* expression makes every would-be wooer despair.'

'I know ... but I want an authentic tie,' I breathed heavily. 'I can't explain it, but this market-place game isn't for me.'

My sister rolled her eye-balls.

'Look at Mum and Dad? Married for twenty-six years and they still sit beside one another on the sofa and cuddle.'

My ways – or outlook – are not very girlish or flirtatious I know, but I will explain the reason for this later in the story.

I drove the Polo down to the hamlet of Cumberford in Gloucestershire, parked near the bowls club, then took the path edged with uncut grass and poppies out towards open furrowed fields.

Stephanie Norman's cottage was old and skewed, built of iron-hard oak beams infilled with herring-bones of burnt brick, yet cosy inside.

In my gap year, before going up to university, I had spent four months on a surveillance course and then as 'Freya' had had Stephanie as my M.I.5 contact during my time at Newcastle.

Stephanie was single, in her forties and quite screw-ball in a job where you perhaps needed to be a bit screw-ball.

She stirred the tea-pot. 'I hear you're engaged to an Edinburgh film director, Sophie?'

'No. That fell flat,' I huffed, 'but he gave me a small part in a film.'

'Title?'

'*A Surfeit of Devils.*'

She cut two sectors from a chocolate and orange cake. 'So, Oxford University? And you fancy working for us again?'

'I'm open to it, yes.'

'A number of our more traditional bosses have recently been "retired" and stock of – shall we say – "less tangibly evident integrity" moved in.'

'Who might betray us to "interested parties"?'

She nodded. 'So we have to bear this in mind in whatever we are doing.'

'The world's full of bods who are good at dissembling. You can never quite join up the dots but you sense their disingenuousness.'

Stephanie added milk to her tea.

'Both Imogen – this girl I'm to befriend – and her tutor, a Dr Cummings, have had to face cliques of quasi-judicial ideologues, whose hidden purpose is to throw them out.'

'Simon Cummings?'

'Yes.'

'He was an Anglican cleric ... until given the boot.'

'So ... a bit of a rebel?'

'More of a *contra*-rebel. He refused to be corralled into their liberal circus or to "dance round the golden calf" as he put it.'

I started on my cake, not forgetting to use the cake-fork.

'My tutor in Newcastle said how Orwellian Oxford is become.'

'Hmm. "Orwellian" has come to mean "like '1984'" rather than "in the style of George Orwell".'

'Or if you're indifferent then perhaps you're, "Oh-well-ian"?'

This tickled her and she sipped her tea.

'This orange cake's very tasty.'

'One pound twenty from the village shop. Roderick compares his new service boss to a peeled orange.'

I looked puzzled.

'The bit with the pith in has been thrown away.'

I mused. 'White rice would be a similar analogy. The husks of the brown are discarded, leaving a less nutritious grain?'

'Enormous kennels and feeble tiny dogs ... that's modern government.'

'May I go off at a tangent?'

'Yes ... or a cosine if you prefer?'

'Speaking of "orange", a week ago some fellow died in northern Northumberland and the papers say that a very expensive, bright orange sports car with a black roof – a Lotus Evora 400 – was spotted nearby in Wooler, owned by a "distinguished Q.C." Could this be a Mervyn Grieff?'

Stephanie, with her access to a number of restricted government sites, went to her computer. 'Yes. Mervyn Grieff Q.C. does own such a car.' She read from an on-line newspaper. 'A local farmer saw it ... and jotted down its number.'

'Thank you.'

'The deceased, one Tayeb Hafid, was a superintendent in the Metropolitan Police.'

I inhaled some cake crumbs and coughed.

'His death is described as "unusual".'

I drank tea to clear my throat. 'Has it gone before the coroner yet?' A ruling of 'death by misadventure' for instance, would tidy it up quite neatly.

'Er ... yes. Yesterday. He returned an "open verdict".'

Back in her armchair, Stephanie spoke softly. 'I saw *A Surfeit of Devils* in Cheltenham with my mother. I thought you were good ... rugged, deep ... and it had an obscure twist embedded in it.'

'Did it?'

'No, but that *was* the twist.'

It sounded like a paradox. I eyed the third-eaten cake whimsically.

'Between ourselves, I have a family interest in Oxford.'

'Oh?'

'My brother Gerard's married to a Jewish lass, Judith Amos, a bio-chemistry lecturer and ... she's been subjected to a number of attempts to blacken her ... '

No second slice of cake seemed to be in the offing.

'Do you want a second driving licence?'

'It might be useful.'

'What name?'

'Er ... Leia Owens?'

She smiled. 'All right ... and we'll give it the address in Dursley.'

As wayfarers in a muddled and crooked world, we shook hands briefly and parted.

*   *   *   *

So, I was on square one of the snakes and ladders board, yet was not too fearful.

In Greek mythology, the younger gods – Apollo, Athena and the 'in' gang – think they are the future. They are serene, look so pure, strike brave poses. They may disguise themselves as swans say, to secretly rape some poor Spartan maid and think it amusing, but do not be deceived; this will not end up in Arcady.

The Furies are far, far older. They are scary and ugly, but they are the ancient lore which cannot be broken ... and which will always come back to bite.

CHAPTER TWO

A colourful oil painting of the Newcastle and North Shields Railway's Carliol Square station popped up on my computer screen and I clicked the 'buy' button.

It was too late to reach Chipping Norton before the gallery closed that day, but Eirig, my cousin – who works on and adores railways – lives in Stroud.

He was delighted to see me and after a kiss we sat down on the sofa in his slightly topsy-turvy flat.

Thirty-one and in scruffy clothes, he none the less looked clean and his hair and nails were neatly trimmed.

When eighteen and on a trip on a train on a preservation railway, he and another lad had climbed onto the carriage roof. The train had then gone under a bridge. The other lad died and Eirig ended up with a metal plate in his skull, a droopy left eyelid and a minimal degree of mental impairment.

I felt entirely at ease with him. With blood-relatives – even if seldom seen – there is a quiet warmth, an unspoken trust.

'Do you have a girlfriend?'

'I did, Lodes ... and was fond of her, but she left me for this suave, hedge-fund analyst.'

'Why?'

He shrugged. 'He had a metallic purple Lamborghini ... but his notions of fun were limited to, "Let's open a bottle of wine and watch a film." He had no hobbies, no interests ... except money.'

I understood this. 'Hobbies matter ... music, tennis, coin collecting ... '

'Not the brightest candle ... but he'll take her to "see the world."'

'Wasps in bottles.'

He heated up a pasta meal-for-two and poured two glasses of fizzy apple juice.

I gave him an unguarded smile. 'Do you feel lonely now?'

'No. I'm alone a lot, but I never *feel* lonely.' He waved a hand at a large and very pretty rag-doll which sat on a wooden chair. 'I sometimes talk to Ceinlys.'

'Oh? She looks happy.'

'She's such a sweetie ... and very coy.'

'I'm glad she doesn't talk back.'

'Uncle Hywel found her in a "reduced to clear" bin on a cross-channel ferry twenty-eight years back ... but she's landed on *terra firma*.'

I sprinkled some Parmesan onto my pasta.

'I've landed a job in Oxford ... so perhaps we can see one another more often?'

'Oh that'll be lovely! What's the job?'

'A research assistant.'

'Researching what?'

'The Newcastle and North Shields Railway.'

'Ah, railways,' he sighed with ecstasy. 'You can come with me to my signal-box one day.'

I grinned. 'I would like that.'

I am five-foot seven and a half and a little broad in the shoulders and hips, such that some have described me as 'bonny'. My hair – which is fair – refuses to grow much beyond shoulder-length and is usually bound as two short stubby sheaves, one either side of my head. My face is round, pale pink, with its cheeks pitted from my using some chemically over-strong blusher.

I heard a dog woof, as it left the flat opposite.

'Horrid dog! Last week it grabbed Ceinlys by the arm, dragged her across the landing and was about to chew her ... till I pounced on it.'

'Do you take Ceinlys out?'

'Sometimes ... to the supermarket. She likes to sit in the trolley. If I took her anywhere else, people might think I was crazy.'

'Why should they not think that in the supermarket?'

He sighed deeply. 'A glass of Taylor's port?'

'Please.'

We had last met two years before, at a funeral.

'As to Lodes, it hurts me to say it, but ... I think the fondness was all one way?'

'If money's her yardstick, you're well rid of her.'

He groaned.

'Making money is not wrong *per se*, but it matters *how* you make it. Does a hedge-fund system analyst actually contribute anything to society?'

'No.'

'Adam Smith says, "Making money is good for society," but there's a caveat, "by productive labour".'

'So not pushing silly bits of paper round a desk?'

'Quite.'

We studied a picture of a Cambrian Railways' engine, our heads almost touching.

'It's crossing a Howe truss girder bridge.' Our temples bumped one another as we examined this bridge minutely.

Beside the line was a pile of surplus ballast. 'Ballast

needs to be large and jagged so that it locks together and does not disperse.'

Our shoulders touched and I sensed a strange tingling. 'Smooth pebbles do not adhere to one another?'

'No.'

I felt the top of his head and the scar hidden under his hair.

Our port and truffles ended, we stood up and exchanged a second quick kiss and cuddle before I left.

I had driven for barely ten miles, when my phone pinged with a coded message. Stephanie wanted me to call her.

I pulled up in a side-road.

'Where are you?'

'Between Stroud and Cirencester.'

'Can you go to Oxford?'

'Er ... yes.'

'Go to a take-away called *The Grasshopper*. It's in Anson Street. Try to see if it looks suspicious. The police say it's above board, but I don't trust them.'

'Will do.'

It was ten to eight when I parked in the next street to Anson Street.

Uncle Hywel had left in the Polo's glove-box a cracked pair of sun-glasses and a dog-eared scrap of paper with a quote from Micah.

I put on the sun-glasses.

There was no queue of customers. I wandered in and looked at the lack-lustre menu pasted onto the back wall.

'A number twenty-two please?'

'That's off. We've no chicken.'

'Oh, then I'll have a number fourteen.'

'That's off too.'

'You seem to have less food here that I have in my kitchen at home?'

I received in reply, 'Oh just,' followed by the most commonly used two-word obscenity.

The European-looking guy behind the counter was covered in purple spots and broad-based pimples, indicative of blood poisoning. His short-sleeved 'Kung Fu' T-shirt enabled me to see the inner aspects of his left elbow and forearm, which were speckled with red dots and blue bruises. A hefty fellow of Asian extraction opened a side-door minimally and Cyclops-like, gave me a one-eyed and unpleasant eye-balling.

I rang Stephanie. 'It's a money-laundering front for a drug racket.'

'Thanks. I suspect it's something else as well, but still, that's a start. It's to do with Judith.'

I went to the police station in Saint Aldate's. 'Hullo. *The Grasshopper*? In Anson Street? It's a money-laundering front for a drug gang.'

A suave young sergeant, with a neat moustache, rested his palms on the desk. 'It's been quite recently investigated by a detective inspector ... and nothing suspicious came to light.'

'Oh. Did he leave his guide-dog outside?'

Our eyes were on the same level and we looked hard at one another for some seconds.

Then he spoke very softly. 'We've been told not to interfere.'

'Why?'

'We do not wish to create further disturbances.'

'Oh? Is not turning a blind eye also a wrong-doing?'

'I'm not aware of such a law.'

I just shook my head, but thought, 'God will judge that also.'

The 'Welcome' mat in the police station entrance lay reversed, so that on leaving you were 'welcomed' back to a straighter world.

Bribery was a possibility, but outside London it was more likely that the inspector would fear an accusation of racial harassment, then before a panel of craven appeasers he would be charged with 'misconduct' leading to dismissal and the possible forfeiture of his pension; a very big gun to the head.

I went back to Anson Street to see if anyone else was naïvely trying to buy food.

From an alley-way a hundred yards distant, I watched a girl with violently shaking legs exit, clutching something in her hand. 'You poor stupid girl,' I muttered to myself.

If they suspect a user of being an *agent provocateur*, they will insist that he take his 'fix' there and then, so that he has no evidence on him on leaving.

I thought of my lovely Mid-Wales. Birds, wild flowers, sheep; playing with a toy train or a lovely rag-doll; all these have a truth about them made stronger by contrast to this underworld of sullied ghoul-like sub-humanity.

The thin, drawn, unhappy girl staggered past me. I so wanted to say something or do something to help her, but could not.

These drug dealers need to be dragged out, put against a wall and shot.

Suddenly a black BMW with heavily tinted windows

skidded to a halt in front of the take-away and three youths leapt out. As the spotty fellow tried to bolt the door, they kicked it in, grabbed him and stuck a knife into his chest.

As the attackers sneered at their collapsing victim, five or six toughies from the resident gang charged down an open stone staircase at the side of the building, intent on seizing their rivals, who then tried to jump into their car and drive off. As the car started to move though, its doors automatically locked before the third youth had opened one and leapt aboard. He was promptly knocked to the ground and hacked at by two machete-wielding savages.

I rang Stephanie again.

'Syed Husaini, the owner, comes from the Bihar region of India,' she said, 'noted for its criminals. He's a local councillor too and he wears a gold watch said to have cost sixty-thousand pounds.'

Three years before, Megan and I had won a magazine competition; a fortnight in Japan.

Eating and drinking there were forbidden on underground trains to avoid crumbs or spillages. A student's soup flask had started to leak and to drip broth. Aghast, he had removed his T-shirt, mopped the floor of the carriage and then used it to soak up the continuing dribbles from his broken flask. When his T-shirt began to reach saturation point, he started sucking it, to restore some absorptive capacity to it; so strong in Japan is their deference to etiquette and to the rules of good behaviour.

I spent the night in a guest house, where before bed I said my prayers. God is light. In Him there is no darkness. Our ways on earth are never wholly pure, yet I know that good is stronger than evil.

Lucinda Elliot's house was a spacious mid-Victorian villa just under a mile from Oxford's city centre.

As I walked up the short gravelled drive, I noted its grey-yellow brickwork with square stone quoins at its corners and chamfered ones around its windows. It was quite narrow but tall, with a steeply gabled roof. Its front door, also tall and with a Gothic arch had two worn stone steps.

Dusty, her teenage daughter, greeted me and led me up the steel fire-escape at the side to see the attic flat.

It was clean and adequate.

'Mum doesn't want students in it. They often give trouble.'

'Did Imogen live here at all?'

'No. She came to tea once or twice when she first arrived in Oxford, but we haven't seen her now for ... six months?'

'What's she like?'

'Quiet. She talked a bit about some hagiography she was reading ... Christine of Bolsena.'

'So she's quite religious?'

'I guess so.' Dusty beckoned me into the long country-style kitchen of the main house for tea.

In the wide hallway a nude female figure sat on a tall stained wooden block. She was two-thirds life-size, cast in bronze and covered in a bluey-green verdigris. Her elegant hands were above her head adjusting her hair. Her neck and arms were slender, her face delicate and her waist improbably narrow. Her left knee was raised as her left heel rested on the edge of the wooden cube. Her wide well-shaped thighs were apart enough such that her vulval cleft was semi-visible. Her breasts were small but pointed. She was decidedly erotic.

'Her name's Tanit. The original's in the Louvre.'

'Phoenician?'

'I think so. From Sidon or Byblos, Mum said.'

I sat down at the long wooden table.

'Does your mother work at the University?'

'Who doesn't round here?' she puffed. 'Professor of European Politics.'

I nodded non-committally.

'She was bent on coming to Oxford, but her school careers master told her she didn't cut the mustard. He suggested Hull, to which she rasped, "Where?"'

I smiled. 'She was not worried by how tough it might be amongst these supposed high-fliers?'

'No.' Dusty poured the tea and found some hob-nob biscuits.

'So she made it ... as an undergraduate?'

'At that time the least popular course was theology, so she applied for it and had luckily done religious studies – I think because of a dishy scripture master – and Latin ... and got in.'

'Oh. Have you thought about your own future yet?'

'I think somewhere like Hull might be more my cup of tea. I've had enough of all the up-themselves snobs around here.'

'I read general arts at Newcastle ... and was happy enough there.'

Dusty nodded seriously.

As I stood up to leave, I handed her a retainer for the flat and probed, 'Matthew seems quite well off ... unusual for a university academic?'

'His father owned a lot of land in Cumbria.'

'Oh.'

'When he died, some distant relatives – including Mum – tried to contest the will.'

'But without success?'

'Matthew's solicitor sent out a snotty letter, saying that only Matthew and his brother were to inherit.'

'And this nasal mucus did the trick?'

Dusty gave a tongue-in-cheek smile and I left.

In Chipping Norton, the painting depicted a scene at an early railway station. Two men in frock-coats and top hats and three ladies with full-length, wide, brightly coloured dresses and three-quarter coats stood on a low stone unroofed platform. The backdrop consisted of a crimson and maroon carriage with 'FIRST' painted on its wooden panels in gold and in the distance, a vague outline of a shed with some packing-cases and a goods wagon. The signature read, 'E. Flower, 1840.'

'He's not in the standard reference books,' admitted the portly owner of *The Decius Gallery*.

'It's the scene which interests us.'

'It's a bit happy-go-lucky, though the overall images come through well ... with just a hint of blurring.'

He found a second, badly water-damaged painting. It was beyond repair, but it showed a third-class carriage, the station name-board 'Wallsend' and again 'E. Flower, 1840'.

'Ten pounds?'

I nodded an affirmative.

Being the summer holiday, most students were down and so Oxford was quite quiet in spite of a sprinkling of tourists.

I entered Exeter College wearing a navy blue skirt, a white blouse and a darkish pink bolero; quite good I thought.

Outlined by the light from the mullioned window of his study, Matthew seemed stooped and even more than before the learned scholar from days of yore.

He was flabbergasted. 'I've never seen a painting of this railway. This will definitely form the front cover, but ... ' he looked at me closely, 'What's happened to your eye?'

It had now gone from the purple to the yellow and lilac stage, as the trapped blood cells broke down.

'I slipped over in the swimming pool.'

We went to *The Grand Café*, which is said to stand on the site of the oldest coffee-house in England, which opened there in 1650. Its décor if a little faded was reminiscent of *La Belle Époque*.

'The Newcastle and North Shields Railway received its Act of Parliament on mid-summer's day, 1836. It opened in 1839 and was taken over by the Newcastle and Berwick in 1844.'

'So a very time-circumscribed subject?'

The tea and poached eggs on toast arrived and I remarked on the promisingly strong orange colour of the yolks.

'Circumscribed?' He considered. 'Dipping toes into needless ponds disturbs the mind. We do not need to fret or have opinions about the world's endless idiosyncrasies or foibles.'

I poured the tea. 'So don't be diffuse?'

'Just accept them and devote yourself to your own tasks. This, the Stoics say, is the way to peace and to wisdom.'

'Matthew, did you ever marry?'

'No. I had a grave disappointment when I was twenty – my eternal love – and railways to a degree, are the substitute for her.'

I eyed him doubtfully and he chortled softly.

I sighed. 'As to boys, I too have only failures to report.'

'I'm sorry if we've let you down?'

I gave him an ambiguous smile. 'Anyway, the eggs are perfect.' I sprinkled a little more salt on mine.

'You'll find someone.' He opened his phone. 'Here is my current sweetheart.'

I guessed the answer, but did not intend to spoil his little joke.

It was a photo of his toy railway.

I gazed at it genially.

His spacious upstairs bachelor pad – also in Canterbury Road – had a quiet, peaceful ambience.

He showed me a few pieces of the two-inch gauge model railway he had made. 'This is a second-class carriage of the N. and N.S.R.' It had a light brown colour scheme with gilded numbers and weighed – I guessed – close on two pounds. 'The thirds were open, pale green and without doors, but I had not discovered the livery used for the first-class ones.'

'Though the painting now solves that?'

'Indeed.'

'Very solid,' I remarked, replacing the wooden and brass four-wheeled carriage back onto the track.

On the sofa, I thumbed a copy of *Early Railway Signalling* until Matthew brought in the coffees and choccies.

'Do you remember that grid reference? Well someone died close by.'

'Oh?' I said with surprise.

'The newspaper said he had a blue and orange scarab brooch pinned to his penis.'

I frowned. 'Strange? Was he Egyptian?'

'No. Tunisian. And he had some metal-detecting equipment.'

'Not fixed to his penis?'

'I assume not ... but a giant cocaine crystal under his foreskin.'

'Oh. That sounds uncomfortable?' I thought for a moment. 'What was he looking for?'

'This crime reporter suggested stolen bars of precious metal.'

'Oh.'

Matthew shrugged. 'Perhaps they'll embalm him and inter him in a sarcophagus?'

'Lucky I didn't go.'

His humour had risen over the past hour and as I prepared to leave, he said with a twinkle, 'Boys are more abstract, more philosophical; girls more practical, immediate, everyday ... cook the dinner, make the sitting-room comfy ... liven us up.'

I gave a 'perhaps' type shrug.

'We'll make a good team.'

*   *   *   *

As I set off down Woodstock Road to Saint Giles – where I had left my car – I passed a mini-supermarket.

On their outside display were some red-currants and I am quite fond of these.

A young shop assistant stood in the doorway, trying to block a fat oaf from leaving. 'I can hear jars clinking in your bag. I want you to open it.'

As he tried to bulldoze his way past her, I grabbed his upper arm and said firmly, 'Do what she tells you.'

An older gentleman drew up too and the shop-lifter reluctantly lowered his bag. From it we extracted ten large jars of coffee.

An ugly copper-haired lass watched us over the magazine she was holding; its cover splashed with *Skimpy Sizzling Bikinis*.

The manager rang the police, but they were too busy dealing with a string of hate crimes.

'Still, we've recovered the coffee,' said the brave little shop-girl.

I bought a tub of the red-currants and sat outside on a bench to eat them.

The ugly lass, sat on a low wall across the street, jabbing away at the buttons of her telephone.

I set off, but after two hundred yards a group of seven youths coming from the town, trotted up to me.

Two girls and a boy – I guessed by their 'Stop Oil' T-shirts – were students, whilst the other four looked rougher.

They grabbed me and pushed me against an old brick wall, overhung by unpruned bushes.

I am pretty spirited, but what can you do against seven? I managed to stay upright and fend off some blows. My shins received kicks, my hair was pulled, I was spat at and a number of punches made it in between my raised forearms.

After a minute or so, the tallest girl ended it and scowled, 'Just take this as a warning.'

Although trembling, I set off for the Welsh coast.

After a seemingly endless journey, Megan laid me down on the sofa and examined my bruised limbs. I sniffled and sobbed; a delayed reaction.

'This girl who phoned her mates ... I think she knew who I was?'

'How could she know that?'

'I don't know ... but I don't think it was about the shop-lifting.'

'Matthew's probably applied to register you?'

I recalled Stephanie's warning about the Civil Service.

Uncle Hywel dropped by.

Stiff, aching and in shock, I stayed horizontal.

Megan made tea and cheese on toast for us and I narrated what had happened.

He eyed me with a sympathetic yet questioning look.

'This job in Oxford,' I hiccoughed, 'it is in part research – which is above board – but it also involves helping a girl who's being picked on ... both – it seems – for her Christian beliefs and her exceptional artistic ability.'

'And it's turning out to be very dangerous,' put in Megan.

I nodded weakly. 'There is risk with it ... yet I feel I should do it,' I snivelled.

He took my limp hand for some seconds. 'Yes, I can imagine ... Oxford. So-called "brilliance" without faith ...

in an ebb-tide which will strand every sturdy or seaworthy boat.'

Megan took away our plates.

'Lie back and I'll tell you a story.'

I did so.

'Josiah, King of Judah, was the only good apple in a long string of bad ones. Manasseh and Amon – his predecessors – lay buried in the Garden of Uzza in the palace grounds in Jerusalem. Uzza, an Arabian goddess, was one of the idols to whom these apostates had burnt incense and so brought down ruin upon the land.'

Oddly spell-bound, I floated in and out of glimpses of this ancient world.

'Josiah removed Baal's golden vessels and the hideous Asherah pole from the temple and broke them in pieces. He tore down the altars on the "high places" after burning the bones of their pagan priests on top of them. He destroyed the dwellings of the male cult prostitutes. He slew the wizards and seers ... '

I gave a faint laugh. 'He sounds like a busy chap?'

'He did everything which God told him, yet, so great was the Almighty's anger with their idol-worship, that still He gave them over to their enemies, who slew them.'

Megan poured two tots of brandy and a black-currant juice for Uncle Hywel and broke a chocolate bar into squares.

The door-bell rang and Megan – a touch taken aback – ushered in a police inspector.

He introduced himself; 'Inspector Jones.'

'Good evening, Inspector.'

'Miss Hughes, were you in Woodstock Road in Oxford today, at around a half past two?'

'Yes.'

Megan added, 'Being beaten up by a posse of thugs.' She pointed to the cuts and bruises on my legs and arms.

'Oh? Did you then see *them* being attacked?'

'No.'

'Two soldiers gave them a number of quite serious injuries.'

I dimly recalled two squaddies entering the Oxfam Bookshop in Saint Giles.

'My oppo in Oxford thinks that these young persons had taunted the soldiers, who then over-reacted.'

I just loved this word 'over-reacted'. I mentioned the two soldiers, but did not mention the bookshop – in case they had purchased anything there – and instead of their maroon berets – which would signify paratroopers – gave them navy ones.

When he had gone, I said, 'This proves that that girl knows who I am.'

Megan raised her glass. 'At least somebody has some guts.'

'Unlike modern clergy,' I said hoarsely, 'who just hold open the gates for all these anti-Christian and anti-free-speech "thinkers".'

Uncle Hywel said, 'If you talk egotistically and tell God what he should do, you're just wasting your breath. The worth of words lies only in the truth behind them.'

I slept soundly that night, still on the sofa. Megan had put a quilt over me.

CHAPTER THREE

The Welsh pageant *Y Tywysog* was enacted one balmy evening in the courtyard of Harlech Castle.

An historical satire, it oozed caricatures and naff jokes. We waved flags, slipped poison into each another's goblets, fought with swords, read from scrolls, fell rapturously in love and gained kingdoms by treachery.

I played Robert the Irn-Bruce, Mary Queen of Scotch, Owain the Sour and Hotty Hotspur.

My black eye had now faded.

Illumined by old carbon-arc footlights and in front of a red and yellow banner and grey plywood battlements, I and my five fellow players bowed to the ninety or so locals and tourists whose enthusiastic clapping we had definitely earnt.

A girl walked up onto the stage with a large bouquet of white lilies.

'For me?' Surprised, I blushed and curtsied.

After a little extra applause, the audience dispersed.

As I wiped my grease-paint off in the small green marquee – which served as our dressing-room – Matthew entered in a T-shirt and long shorts.

'You were superb.'

I smiled happily. 'Thank you ... and thank you too for the lovely flowers.'

'I a quarter-followed the translation.'

The call-boy ushered in the florist's girl. 'Thirty-two pounds, please Sir.'

Matthew found two twenty-pound notes.

'I don't have any change.'

'Oh don't worry. Keep it.'

'Oh, thank you!' She gave me a sly look. 'I hope she's worth it.'

I laughed. 'Unexpected generosity always pleases.'

Matthew placed a folder on the trestle-table beside a small silvered metal mirror. 'Sophie, comb through this; registration forms and such.'

I nodded.

He seemed in good spirits. 'I think Roderick's advice was good.'

I guessed that he saw me as fairly feet-on-the-ground; not some cliché-soaked air-head. 'Well ... let's not count chickens too soon?'

After he had left, Huw, our producer came up to me. 'Sophie, a rather odious fellow – mid-thirties, flashily dressed – has been asking where you live?'

'You didn't tell him?'

'Of course not.'

Changing my sandals for shoes and tugging on a jacket, I set off for home, carrying my bouquet and a carrier-bag full of bits and bobs. I walked down the steep twisting lane known as Twtil to the bottom of the castle rock where my parents' little house stood near the railway.

The inky-blue sky was clear, the air still, whilst an unobscured and watchful three-quarter moon scattered her glitter across walls and hedges.

Suddenly I heard muffled footsteps behind me, so rounding a hair-pin, I slipped through an open gate.

Crouching down behind a rowan bush, I watched as a soft-footed spectre trod by then stopped.

After a *sotto voce* curse, this blurry shape turned and retraced its steps. I shadowed it until in Stryd Fawr it opened the passenger door of a long silvery-grey coupé – with its hood up – and climbed in. The last piece of anatomy to be drawn aboard – glimpsed in the haze of a feeble street-light – was the curved slender leg of a young woman, beneath the hem of a red coat.

This black-topped, grey U.F.O. then glided smoothly off.

*   *   *   *

Two days later, as the misty dawn receded before the gold-tinted blues and greens of another summer's day, Megan and I returned from paddling in the sea, to see a red and black 250 c.c. trials bike draw up outside our old pre-fab.

We had caught a big crab, so I took it inside and started to set out the breakfast things, whilst Megan stayed to watch the rider dismount and tether her helmet to the bike's pannier rack.

'Hullo?'

'Are you Sophie Hughes?'

'No. She's inside. And you are?'

'Emma Hyman.'

This girl – of about my own age – entered via the kitchen door which stood open. She tapped, but did not wait for a response.

I stopped drawing two big eyes on the crab's upper shell and put down my blue felt-tip pen.

'Hi. I'm Emma. I understand that Matthew Sleight's asked you to do research for him?'

'Excuse me? What business is this of yours?'

'That depends. What's your *rôle*?'

'Umm ... research assistant.'

'Researching what?'

'Er ... a railway.'

'His field is early Scandinavian languages.'

As she cast a deprecating glance around our shabby kitchen, Megan eyed me from behind Emma's back, then exited inconspicuously.

'The railway book is not a university project.'

'All right, but anything else? Any subterfuges ... or other covert dabblings?'

I was too dumbfounded to reply.

After a prolonged stare, she demanded, 'Well?'

'Er ... no.'

'Good.' She flashed me a smile. 'Then all's well ... but if you are up to something, it will go badly for you.'

It dawned on me that I had glimpsed her in the audience at the castle ... in a shiny, bright red coat.

With an upturned nose she glanced around our outdated abode for a second time.

'Do you like it?'

She strode out and – in her leather jeans and half-unzipped canvas jacket – jumped astride her motorcycle, pulled on her gloves and attempted to kick-start it. After five humiliating failures, she thumped the petrol tank.

Emma was quite attractive I guess, but spoilt by her arrogance.

Megan strolled down to the kerb. 'The ignition cable's come off the spark-plug.'

Emma glared at her, then down at the loose cable,

clipped it back on, tried one more kick-start and her bike burst into life.

She whispered huskily, 'Did you do that?'

Megan did not reply.

'Don't cross swords with me.'

Megan closed up to her. 'Then *don't* threaten my sister.'

'Oh just buzz off ... you sad little Welsh witch.'

I was now close by and our neighbour Dafydd had stopped painting his front railings to watch.

Emma with narrowed eyes, squinted at the sun, engaged first gear and moved off.

As she did a U-turn, her front wheel skidded sideways in some loose gravel and her bike went from under her.

Breathing heavily she stood up, righted her bike, remounted and – after an inaudible oath – rode off more warily.

'She'll have bruised that hip.'

'How does *she* know I'm working for Matthew?'

'Lucinda?'

I inhaled. 'I wouldn't think so? She struck me as being quite unhappy.'

We went in for breakfast.

'Where's that crab?'

It was half-way into the sitting-room.

'Perhaps it wants to watch telly?'

At seventeen, Megan is six years younger than I. A touch above medium height and quite slender, her smooth oval face suggests a nature more well-disposed and blithe than it actually is.

'Why doesn't Romeo come and call? I've dropped two or three hints.'

45

'And why do stunning girls always fall for utter bone-heads?'

'Do they?' she asked, then – on seeing it to be a tease – shook her head.

I waved an open palm. 'I rest my case.'

She gave me two fingers, smiled drily, then went off to run a couple of errands for our old neighbour, Eirwen.

*   *   *   *

In Newcastle-upon-Tyne's City Library, I copied a map dated 1841, on which the fledgeling railways of the time were shown. The girl who helped me also found a pink and purple woodcut print of the Ouseburn viaduct during its construction.

'You could change it back to black and white if you don't like its psychedelic colours?'

I also tracked down two articles from local, early Victorian newspapers on Matthew's list.

After booking into a hotel near York, Megan rang to say that Emma Hyman had re-surfaced.

'Why?'

'I don't know, but whatever the intent, it went wrong.'

Storm clouds had gathered during the afternoon and a sudden cloud-burst had greeted her arrival. Perhaps it blurred her visor, for in stopping at the edge of our road, she misjudged the ragged tufts of grass and slithered into a ditch. It was the scream of her bike's engine as she tried to free it, which alerted Megan.

Soaked and unable to extricate her bike, she had sheltered under a tree.

As the rain eased off, a passing police car drew up and Constable Gruffydd rang her recovery service for her.

Megan said that Emma had seen her watching from a window. Would this second rout convince her that Megan really was a witch?

The York Railway Museum possessed an early hand-written ticket of the N. & N.S.R., which they allowed me to photograph. It is a superb museum and I was struck with the three earliest surviving railway carriages in the world; four-wheelers from the 1830s; the third-class one just an open box with wooden seats.

Unpicking the building of a canal or a railway say, shows how much effort and invention have gone into shaping our modern world.

Back in Harlech, Megan insisted we go to *The Simple Milkmaid*. This pub had been *The Turk's Head*, but since historically a 'Turk' meant a Moslem, they had been told to rename it.

We ordered spiced meat-balls with spaghetti at the bar, then found a table. The carpet belched every time you trod on it. Enough alcohol had been spilt on it such that bubbles were fermenting beneath it.

Gwyn Gruffydd entered in civvies. We had been at school together.

'Sophie! What are you up to these days?'

'Er ... I've a job in Oxford.'

'Oh? Going up in the world?'

'All that glitters is not gold.'

'True.'

Megan asked, 'Yesterday, that girl with the motorcycle ... what was the upshot?'

'She was limping, so we removed her left boot. Her ankle was swollen and the lower end of her fibula seemed to be bent outwards.'

'Oh.'

'So we put her motorcycle into the police compound and summoned an ambulance.'

Our food number was called and Gwyn moved off.

At the bar, the carpet having burped again, I asked, 'When are you going to replace this threadbare thing?'

'We're becoming a tandoori chicken house dear ... so it'll soon be tiles.'

'Oh.'

My friend Delyth squinted at me. 'Parents away for five weeks? Life's so unfair.'

Our dish was tasty enough.

'So no Romeo?' I whispered to Megan. 'For heaven's sake, try another trout pond.'

She pinched my last meat-ball.

'Rotter!'

Next afternoon, with a box of liqueurs, I entered Bangor Hospital's orthopaedic ward and pulled a chair up beside Emma's bed. 'May I?'

She managed a crinkle-cut smile. Her left leg was in a below-knee plaster and elevated.

'Screwed or just manipulated?'

'The former.'

'Megan then put just the right mix of ingredients into her cauldron?'

'I'm sorry if I seemed a bit off the other day ... I'm having trouble with my love life.'

'Oh.' I awaited enlightenment.

'How close are you to Matthew?'

I was puzzled. 'What do you mean?'

'Would you be prepared to do something, er ... "surreptitious"?'

'Like what?'

She gave me a long hard look. 'Can't you guess?'

'Whatever it is you're suggesting, the answer's "No."'

She sighed like one dealing with a difficult child. 'Have you heard of Professor O'Rourke?'

'No.'

'He would be prepared to reward you *very* generously.'

I looked sternly at her and did not answer.

'Well, perhaps we've miscalculated ... or jumped the gun?'

The tea lady was going round. Emma asked for a coffee, then opened the liqueurs, took one herself and offered me one.

'No thanks.'

'Are they laced with cyanide?'

'Does this O'Rourke cove drive a flashy grey coupé?'

Emma's eyes narrowed.

'Are you his bit of fluff?'

She leant her head back and looked up at the ceiling. 'On and off.'

'So sometimes he's on you and sometimes he's off you?'

'That the usual arrangement, isn't it?' She squeezed out a sour grin. 'Anyway, should you change your mind ... '

'All right. I will have a liqueur.' I took one, stood up and left.

At home our parents had returned from Cyprus.

CHAPTER FOUR

Dad is bluff and good-hearted, but cannot be trusted not to repeat colourful anecdotes to his pals. Mum is homely and kind, but would leak any confidences to Dad. Megan and I had learnt long since to keep our own counsels.

'So what's this new job?'

'Academic research in Oxford.'

'So some rubbish statistics?'

'No. It's about an old railway.'

'How much is he paying you?'

'Half a million.'

'What? Ho, ho. Why didn't you take that job with those Indian doctors?'

'Because they were smug and coining money by writing bent medico-legal reports.'

'Shove the marmalade over. Then what about those Chinese import guys?'

'I just didn't like them ... and they felt themselves a bit superior too. They said how wonderful their country and their government were and how crap ours were, but still I noted preferred to live in the West because of its freedoms. I hinted at their hypocrisy and they threw me out.'

'Well, if you're going to Oxford, you need to retire that cardigan.'

Megan, pretending to have caught a fitness bug, was off to the gym again.

'And take your fishing rod,' I advised.

Dad looked bewildered. 'Fishing? You can't fish at the gym?'

I helped mum make a shepherd's pie.

'So this is lamb? Cottage pie uses beef?'

'Yes.'

'Why not call it "cowherd's pie", to be consistent?'

Dad lowered his *Modern Army* magazine. 'Because that would sound like "coward's pie".'

Ah, 'heducaishon', I thought.

Mum asked, 'Any luck on the boyfriend front?'

'Hmm ... '   '

Today it is so tricky. If born a century earlier, I might have been a farm-girl working in a Welsh valley. Perhaps a low-lying one, amid green hills and dotted with ochre-coloured haycocks and black cattle? Or I might have been a weaver's daughter like Mary Jones, saving her pennies to buy a Bible? Or a shepherdess in an upland pass with its mossy crags and lean sinewy sheep?

Oxford, despite its towers topped with green flags or crescent moons, the banners on railings promoting 'anti-whiteness' and its anti-Fascist and animal rights marches, should – none the less – yield something grittier or more scholarly if one delved beneath this garish red-green-blue confetti.

I lay on my bed.

Our lives need to be given in service ... even in servitude. Then we fit in with the creation. Our egos alone are futile, as is a smoke-screen of sociological bunkum. Roman slavey or medieval thraldom were not without their up sides. At least then everyone knew what they were.

Megan returned. 'What are you doing? It's only half past ten.'

'I'm lying on my bed, listening to Bach's double violin concerto.'

'Not listening to Bach's violin concerto whilst lying on a double bed ... and wishing ... '

'Look, Miss Funny ... ' I leapt up and started a tussle, but stopped abruptly. 'Those yobs who attacked me ... revenge is often seen as an external agent – as with the Greek Furies – but it could also be seen as an internal or self-generated punishment?'

'Oh?'

'In that dark deeds bar the way to a truer or wiser spirit?'

'Hmm, something there maybe. Quite good for you.'

'That's all right, an equal division of labour ... you provide the bull.'

Megan took a deep breath.

'Anyway, I'm leaving for Oxford.'

'Term doesn't start for another ten weeks.'

'I know ... but I feel I should be there.'

I loaded up my car, gave everyone a hug and set off.

*　　*　　*　　*

At Lucinda's, again only Dusty was in.

'Mum's in Morocco, but you're invited to afternoon tea next Sunday.'

'That'll be nice.'

She waved at an open magazine. Two Scandinavian girls had wandered off the prescribed tourist beats in Morocco, been raped, murdered and beheaded.

She helped me lug my stuff up to the attic.

'Tea?' she asked.

'Or shall we go out?'

'Yes. That sounds good.'

'I'd like to meet Imogen. Could you introduce me?'

'Mum says I'm not to see her.'

'Why?'

'She didn't say.'

'Could we just not mention it?'

Dusty I learnt, resented being bossed around by her mother.

Whilst she changed and fixed her hair, I thumbed through a book titled *Canaanite Religion*.

'In Tyre the temple of Melkart had a stone outer wall but inside it was of aromatic and perfumed cedarwood. Two pillars held up the roof, one covered in gold and the other in emeralds, which in the gloom and flickering candle-light shone with exquisite beauty. Herodotus wrote of them. The sandalwood altar had palm-tree and pomegranate shapes in bas-relief, inlaid with gold.'

The book's bold and radiant art-work stirred your fantasy, unlike some dry scholarly exposition.

Dusty appeared in a dark-grey dress with an orange bow holding its cleavage together and a thin white anorak.

We walked to Imogen's flat, a further half mile north of the town centre on the corner of Ferry Pool Road. She rented a first-floor apartment in a fairly modern, three-storey block, surrounded by lawns and trees.

We pressed the intercom button.

After a wait came, 'Hullo?'

'Imogen? It's Dusty. Can I see you? I've a friend with me.'

The catch on the main door clicked open.

We climbed the stairs and were admitted via a hallway into Imogen's main room, which if a little bare was clean and comfortable.

She wore an off-white paint-smock, daubed with blue and pink smudges.

Dusty introduced me and explained that I was doing research for her uncle.

On the coffee-table, a Bible lay open at The Book of Ruth and various papers and books were strewn around the floor.

An easel with the beginnings of a painting stood near the glass sliding doors which opened onto the balcony. On it, charcoal outlines showed a girl bent over, gleaning in a field where the reapers had ended their toil.

'We're translating Ruth next term. It's quite pastoral ... almost idyllic ... set in quiet rolling farmland.'

Even at this early stage, I sensed – by an oddly perceptive smile – that Imogen trusted me.

She made no effort to impress, to cut an image or to mimic an exciting persona. She was quiet, thoughtful and wholly natural.

'Only four chapters,' Dusty noted.

'It's set in the days before enmity broke out between Judah and Moab. It describes the barley harvest and their ways of transacting business ... and its characters are rustics, without airs or pretences.'

'I'll reread it,' Dusty affirmed. 'I remember it vaguely ... Ruth the Moabitess and Boaz, a good and honest landowner?'

'Yes. Scripture helps us to see changes as purposeful ... as poignant, rather than as arbitrary?'

Dusty said that we were headed to an Italian restaurant and would she like to join us, but she shook her head.

I touched on a more serious topic. 'Matthew says that

you've suffered some trouble ... from other students?'

She gave a lop-sided smile. 'It's not often ... and I can take it. Besides, I'm not going to cower to those little despots.'

I breathed in slowly. 'That can take courage?'

'To many of them, Christianity is the enemy.'

Dusty quoted from her religious studies' lessons at school, verse twenty-nine from surah nine of the Qur'an. '"When strong enough, you are to fight the infidel and subdue him such that he pays you the *jizya*." This *jizya* seems to be a kind of tribute money ... and so a token of subservience.'

'So it establishes two tiers of citizenship; believers and non-believers?' I queried.

'Yes. And it does not say "fight in self-defence", but just "fight" or "conquer".'

We were silent for a time.

'Pasta perhaps another time?' I suggested.

Imogen nodded and smiled. 'Yes. Perhaps another time.'

Dusty gave her a brief kiss on the cheek and we left.

In *Pinocchio's*, I went to the bar to order before rejoining Dusty at a window table.

'I've ordered the *Picasso*. It looks quite tasty.'

'*Picasso*? Do they drop it on the floor, then put all the pieces back together in the wrong order?'

'That's the one.'

Dusty pointed to a discarded newspaper. 'Listen to this. "Crazy man of the week. Sam N. Hunter, a multi-millionaire from New Jersey, left no money to his daughter as she had not spoken to him for five years. Instead his money was to be used to pay for his lovely rag-doll Sophie to live in a penthouse suite at the local Hilton until the money ran out."'

I laughed. 'Go on.'

'"However the Hilton refused to take her ... " That seems odd? An easy way to make money you would think? "So plan B was for his sister to inherit two thousand dollars a week on condition that she took Sophie for tea at the café in the local park every Sunday."'

'With little china cups and saucers?'

A basket of crusty bread, some butter and a carafe of white Chianti descended. '*Grazie.*'

Dusty recalled, 'Mum and I visited Imogen and her dad some years back. Even then she wished to study at Oxford, though she knew her chances were slim.'

Imogen was five-foot six, slender, erect, with almost no breast or hip curvature and with straight light-brown hair hanging down her back. Her pale, softish, unmarked face was neither especially attractive nor unattractive.

'"Contented" describes Imogen I think ... not so much "happy" as "happy with where she is".'

Dusty asked quietly, 'Could she be a Lesbian?'

'Definitely not.'

'What do Lesbians actually do?'

'I don't know. I'm not one. Matthew compares it to having a toy train set with two tunnels and no train.'

Lucinda rang.

'I'm with Sophie ... in a pizzeria.' The call lasted barely thirty seconds. 'Checking up on me. She likes my smiley face which pops up when she rings. I'm tempted to change it for one with an eye-roll?'

'No, don't wind her up.'

'One large pizza and some salad were lowered onto the table.

Suddenly I saw the fat slob shop-lifter and the bony ugly girl enter. So, they were a pair? He was tossing a lump of toffee into his gob. They sat at the table behind me.

I gave Dusty a watching brief. There were very few customers.

'He's now chomping on a second lump. The path to obesity is paved with discarded sweet wrappers.'

'Living for the moment?'

'This pizza crust's hard. Was *Pinocchio* made of wood?'

'Yes.'

'Unlike Imogen, I'm not sure what to do. I've no real strengths.'

'There's a Japanese saying; "Do not be too delighted with your talents nor too down about your shortcomings, for you know not where the 'it' is leading you."'

'That sounds quite oriental.'

'Buddhist I imagine. Shall we ask for the diamond-edged knives?'

'Arabs by contrast have no curiosity.'

'Marcus Aurelius – who was a Stoic – said that his lack of ability in rhetoric and poetry were a blessing sent by the gods, preparing him for his more sober and difficult task as emperor.'

'You did Japanese at Newcastle?'

'For one year, then swapped to general arts.'

'Their historical quaintness seems like a toy theatre.'

I beckoned to the waitress and asked for two peppermint ice-creams, then turned back to Dusty. 'So how did Imogen manage to come to Oxford?'

'It was a bit of a fluke. The University offered a scholarship for the winner of some big European art competition ... '

'And Imogen won?'

'Yes, so she by-passed all the usual hurdles.' Dusty tapped my shin with her foot. 'The girl's called Poppy ... and the guy has a lisp. Aircraft carriers are apparently "youthleth white helephants".'

'Is he an aircraft carrier then?'

'And now he's dangling a chilli above his mouth, preparing to swallow it whole.'

'Like a dolphin at the zoo, being fed a fish?'

'He's called Steg.'

'I hope it burns a hole in his oesophagus.'

Poppy must have suddenly recognised me because she stood up and came round to our table.

'So it is you? Just understand that the castle has been captured and if you fight, you'll be shot through with bullets and arrows.'

It took me a few seconds to form a response. 'The Byzantines struggled for seven hundred years to hold back chaos.'

'The cultural norms are being reset; end of story.'

I was speechless, but Dusty came to the rescue. 'The Byzantines were still right to fight though, even if they lost?'

There was a brief hiatus.

'Enjoy your Kindergarten ... while it lasts.' Poppy gave us two fingers and stalked off with a hint of stiffness or brazenness.

With her harsh sour face, short coppery hair and a decidedly rough air, her man-appeal – if she had any – would be of the insolently provocative sort.

Dusty finished enucleating the chocolate chips from her ice-cream and we asked for the bill.

'Press this button to add ten per cent for service or that one for twenty,' said the surly young waitress.

'Where's the minus button?'

As we stood up, the fat lisping troglodyte clutched his chest, turned a ghastly blue and muttered, 'Poppy, I'm not well.'.

Dusty and I raised our eyebrows and exited.

As we walked home along Saint Giles and then Woodstock Road, we passed the spot where I had been duffed up. I mentioned it to Dusty and the lead-in parts played by Steg and Poppy.

She looked horrified. 'Actually, there have been a few stories like that recently. You just have to be careful what you say ... or be beaten up.'

'I'm not usually frightened, but ... '

'I would have screamed blue murder ... and hoped someone came.'

'Fights at school were just an ineffectual flailing of arms ... although once I came unstuck with a girl whose dad was a boxer and had given her lessons.'

'Did you report it to the police?'

'No. I doubt it would do any good.'

'It's still a record, even if they only put a line down in their desk ledger.'

'Hmm ... to expect any action there would be no minor conceit.'

Dusty and I parted after quite a friendship-forming evening; she into the main house and I up to my attic.

*   *   *   *

On the last Saturday in July, a rally took place in Oxford promoting open borders and the welcoming of asylum seekers. It consisted mostly of students and older white liberals, who met up in the city centre, many bearing placards.

A young masked Asian man – who may or may not have been with the marchers – spotted Judith Amos as she gazed at a travel agent's window.

He drew a knife. Someone shouted. As she spun round, his blade went into her upper left arm. He would have stabbed her again except for two quick-acting bystanders who grabbed him and threw him to the ground.

Judith had a one-inch-deep wound which someone bandaged tightly and pressed on, to stop it bleeding. She was then taken to hospital where two of the nurses refused to treat her because of her race.

Whilst everyone's attention was elsewhere, the attacker slunk off.

The police, not having responded immediately, later questioned Judith in her hospital bed. 'Did you manage to photograph him? No? Then it's unlikely we'll be able to trace him.' They were quietly relieved not to have to probe anyone from an ethnic minority.

Stephanie rang. 'Can you see if you can find anything out?'

I gazed at internet images of this otherwise peaceful,

three-hundred-strong event. There were very few non-white marchers and only two who fitted the attacker's description. One held a green flag aloft and so could be discounted. The only image of the other was blurred.

The rally organiser was the local secretary of the GAT Union, whose Banbury office was closed over the weekend.

It suddenly struck me that three out of four of the placards were printed; red and yellow and all alike.

Next morning, I went to Cornmarket Street and being a Sunday the litter-bins had not been emptied. I found one of these placards, folded into four, in a bin outside a coffee-shop and took it home.

In tiny print at the bottom it read, 'Printed by N.I.S. Printers, Oxford, England.'

On the Monday, I found this business which occupied the ground-floor of an old shoe factory in Howe Street. I could hear the clatter of printing presses as I walked by under its windows. A cosy little café, *The Brewhaha*, lay across the road, so at noon, I bought a cup of tea and a tea-cake and sat at a window table.

I watched the printing works. Dim figures moved about inside, some parcels were delivered and a caller came and went.

Then a thin older man in a brown smock came out, crossed over to the café and queued before buying a sandwich and a cup of tea.

The place had suddenly become busy and by good fortune he asked if he could sit at my table.

I smiled, waved a hand and said, 'Please.'

He had a newspaper folded in two of a moderately

right-wing persuasion. Its headline read 'Kings of inaction' and it railed against the current government's seeming paralysis.

I leant forward. 'Do you work at the printers across the road?'

'Er ... yes.'

He was in his early fifties and looked a touch depressed. Physically he was what my rotund mother would call 'a ham-bone'.

'May I ask who had those "No Borders Asylum Seekers Welcome" placards printed?'

He looked at me, unsure how to reply. 'Do you belong to some extremist clique?'

'No ... nor do I work for Ernst Blofeld,' I whispered.

He managed a smile and sipped his tea.

'Do I look dangerous? Trust me, please?'

'It's an organisation called STUB,' he murmured.

'Do you have their details?'

He paused and eyed me. 'Umm ... we've an email address, though I've not seen a postal one. A courier came with the order and a cheque and then again to collect the print-run.'

'Oh? They paid by cheque?'

'A bit unusual ... its sort code was 10-00-00; the Bank of England.'

An intriguing detail. A government ministry? Although private accounts are also held there.

I hate offering money, it seems so sordid, but ... 'You couldn't find out the email and those cheque details for me could you? I don't mean to offend, but ... three hundred pounds?'

I suspect the money was not the sole issue for him, but I suppose he thought he might as well take it if it was on offer.

After some prolonged munching, he muttered, 'Tomorrow? Here? Same time?'

I eyed my crossword. 'A game played by frogs, perhaps? Seven letters.'

'Croquet.' He winked, stood up and left.

Next day two envelopes slid past one another across the table, whilst two seeming strangers fought with their bacon-lettuce-and-tomato sandwiches.

'The accounts' girl logged on and then the manager called her to his office,' came out softly with a spray of crumbs, 'so I seized the chance.'

'Well done,' I slurped.

The email began 'STUB', then came five random letters in minuscule, then '666'.

In Cumberford, Stephanie studied the cheque.

N.I.S. had photographed it in order to pay it in electronically and my 'friend' had printed off the image. The account was 'STUB UK' and the 'Authorised signatory' looked like, 'B.A. Elwell'.

Stephanie with an account name, sort code and number, could track its registered postal address.

Her face paled. 'This account's joint; "STUB UK" and "HMGUX04". It has a Whitehall address.'

'So although joint, you can request a cheque book printed for just one party?'

'Yes.'

In the kitchen, as we made tea and toast, I saw that she was uneasy. 'If your search is flagged up, might there be a witch-hunt?'

'Well ... they'll know who the witch is for a start.'

Whilst buttering the toast, I tried to be up-beat. 'They might not notice ... or just let it blow over?'

'Yes ... or they might not.' After a silence she continued, 'If I was younger, I'd move to the States.' She added milk to her cup. 'There's a permanent under-secretary in the Treasury named Beatrice Elwell.'

As intelligence cogs, we come in two sizes. Those like Stephanie, who are government employees, stay back from the action. Informants, such as myself, are in the more forward positions but are supposedly protected by anonymity; referred to only by codenames or ciphers.

Yet there are modern civil servants, who feel strange 'moral obligations' to betray us, claiming we are a threat to the 'civil liberties' of others. Another cohort see it simply as fun to gnaw woodworm-like at the ship's timbers.

Then I remembered O'Rourke's coupé. I had seen it in town and noted its rear window dealership sticker.

Stephanie looked it up. 'Current owner, Gavin Fitzgibbon O'Rourke, acquired April 2018 ... and one previous owner, Achmed Alamgir, acquired April 2018.'

'So ... a gift?' I queried.

As I left, for the first time I gave her a hug.

*   *   *   *

I went to see Judith with a spray of pink roses and some gypsophila.

Observatory Street is lined with small Victorian terrace-houses, all painted in various pastel shades; a bit toy-town.

She asked me in and we sat in the window of their

cramped but cosy little front-room with two cups of tea and a tin of Malted Milk biscuits on the dark-oak gate-leg table.

Judith's features were not strongly Jewish, her hair being medium brown and her nose only a little bulbous near the tip; far less bulky than in most Semites.

Her left upper arm was bandaged.

'Gerard's gone to Israel to look at properties. I had intended to hand in my notice at Christmas and we would leave next summer ... but we've decided to bring it forward and just go as soon as possible.'

'You're certainly safer there than you are here. Did they arrest anyone?'

'A white guy, who shouted some insult about Allah.'

Judith and her husband had no children. Her parents lived in Tel Aviv.

'We plan to buy a bed and breakfast somewhere near Acre or Haifa.' She smiled whimsically. 'Spend the morning tidying the guest rooms and the afternoon selling ice-cream on the beach ... it sounds good doesn't it?'

'It sounds very good.'

'And Gerard's a baker so that's always a second job if we need it.'

I spoke of the likelihood that there had been covert governmental – or at least Civil Service – support for the march.

'Busy scuttling the ship?'

'It seems that's what they want?'

As I left an elderly but sprightly looking gentleman came out of the house next door.

He threw me a crinkly smile. 'How is she? Judith?'

'Tip-top. Alive and kicking.'

'Good. The Normans have been here for four years. We moved in in the same month.'

'Oh.' I wished him well.

As I walked away I felt quite moved by Judith's lack of bitterness. Perhaps this knife-wielding hoodie had done her unintentionally a good turn?

The GAT Union offices were in a modern office block on the outskirts of Banbury; perhaps just half a dozen rooms, but quite plush.

The chubby young fellow on reception paused his computer game and gave me a friendly smile.

'Is Citra Assagaf in?' I asked.

'What's it about?'

'The rally in Oxford ... on Saturday.'

'I'll see.' He vanished briefly. 'She's in the powder room, but can see you in a few minutes.'

Was not Guy Fawkes once caught in the powder room?

'You have to sign in.' He pushed a ledger towards me and asked for some I.D.

I produced my 'Leia Owens' driving licence.

A buzzer buzzed.

'Through that door and second on the right.'

I knocked on the faceless modern beech-veneered door, was called in and offered a seat in a quite sumptuous office.

The woman was about forty, Sino-Tibetan in her features, though of somewhat darker skin colour than the usual Chinese or Japanese citizen.

I explained that I was a friend of the girl who had been stabbed at the rally and wondered if they had any clues as to her assailant.

She gave me a cold smile. 'This is not a detective agency.'

'No, but if you know anything which might identify the offender ... ?'

On her fingers were six gold rings, each with a sovereign embedded, round her neck a heavy gold chain and on a peg an expensive and thick fur jacket.

Her degree certificate was framed on the wall behind her. It was in French and the university – distorted by the glass-reflected light – looked like that of the Sour Bone.

I pointed to it. 'Albert Camus said that freedom is simply a chance to improve yourself.'

She saw me glance at the green cotton pennant mounted on a wooden dowel on a filing-cabinet and would also have seen that round my neck – since today I had on an open jacket, an open-neck blouse and no woolly – I wore a small gold cross on a fine gold chain.

I could see her drawing inferences.

I said softly, 'So ... two levels of justice?' I had no intention of going to ground.

Her smile did not hide her wantonness. 'Soon we are going to rule here ... and your weakness is going to help us.'

A knock on the door was followed by the head of a young man from the Indian sub-continent. 'Do you want coffee serving Citra?'

'No thank you ... and will you show Miss Owens out?'

As we stood up, she whispered, 'And we will desecrate your vile Christian graves.'

It was a lovely day. The sun shone. I drove past a field with some sheep in it and in town bought a cappuccino and an apricot croissant.

I thought of Shakespeare's lines;

Let me embrace thee, sour adversity,
For wise men say it is the wisest course.

Like Lear or Hamlet – though surrounded by troubles – you must not fold. They showed courage and optimism ... and they played their parts boldly until the last curtain fell.

*   *   *   *

In his Canterbury Road flat, I gave Matthew the haul of artefacts from Newcastle and York.

A photo of a pale-looking girl of about twenty, in a lemon-coloured dress, I guessed to be his 'lost love'. Under it was written 'Sally'.

He saw me glance at her and smiled wanly. 'She died when she was twenty-six.' He took a deep breath.

'Have you heard of Emma Hyman?'

'No.'

'She's the mistress of a Professor O'Rourke.'

'Let's heat up some tomato soup. Do you know who he is?'

'No.'

'He's the Master of Newlove College.'

'Oh.' In the kitchen, I added, 'I *think* they wanted me to accuse you of some wrong-doing.'

He nodded as he struggled with the tin-opener. 'Our college heads – whether titled warden, rector, master or whatever – usually have a few achievements behind them ... an Olympic bronze say, won the M.C. whilst serving in the Commandos, discovered a new isotope, ambassador to Chile ... A couple are purely scientific or academic it's true, but O'Rourke seems to have nothing.'

I stirred and salted the soup.

'Make sure it's hot ... and *white* bread ... and butter.'

I nodded.

'These characters are usually colourful, amiable, even if at times – like Aethelred the Unready – they're a touch ineffective.'

'Why should O'Rourke have a bone to pick with you?'

We settled ourselves at the table.

'Four years ago he applied for a post in London as senior lecturer in Scandinavian studies and I was on the selection panel.

One candidate, Catharine Ayre, had spent many years in Norway and when I spoke in Old Norwegian, she fielded it pretty well ... '

'Is that Old Norse?'

'No. Old Norse ends around ten-fifty. Old Norwegian follows until about thirteen fifty.'

'Oh.'

'Most of what Catharine said, the other interviewers pretended they could not understand.'

'So ... rigged?'

'In comes O'Rourke – the blue-eyed boy – very cocky. His linguistic knowledge was quite patchy.'

I dunked half a buttered roll into my soup.

'However, he had pirated an unpublished article from my friend Professor Sims in Durham, translated it into German, altered its title and published it in a Continental periodical under his own name.'

'Goodness ... what a nerve?'

'Such things are not so uncommon. I raised this and said that if they appointed him, I would seek out the vice-chancellor.'

'So Catharine landed the job?'

'No. They chose the third candidate.'

'Lucky fellow. So how is it that this upstart is now Master of Newlove?'

'I don't know.'

'Forged testimonials?'

'Nothing would surprise me.'

Having finished the soup, we relocated to the sitting-room. Its windows looked down onto a garden edged with trees, where two small children played.

'He's definitely not worthy of his current position. It's news though, that he's bisexual.'

'Bisexual?'

'When you meet him, you'll see. He's more camp than a row of tents.'

'Oh. If you bend something enough, perhaps it becomes straight again?'

'His boyfriend's a South African cricket umpire ... so he's always flying off to test matches.'

Matthew uncapped a bottle of Courvoisier, tots of which then glugged into two brandy glasses.

'His car I think, is a gift from a rich sheikh.'

Matthew offered me a chocolate mint.

'So why was Catharine not chosen?'

'There's an Old Swedish poem, *The Battle of Sveinstunga* and some years back articles appeared giving it a symbolic meaning; the blue shields with red bosses were the faces of the Aesir – the Nordic gods – the snowy rock-strewn gorge was Thrymheimr and so on. Then Catharine went to the village of Vektskala on Sweden's northern coast on the Gulf of Bothnia – which has an undeciphered runic stone called "The Sveinsbunga Stone". The topography there – a triple-peaked hill, a split waterfall, an island with a steep cliff at one end – was exactly as described in the poem. So she said it was simply the story of a real battle and so sank all these allegorical theories ... on which one of the interviewers had chiefly founded his reputation.'

We clinked glasses.

'She's now lecturing in Sydney, so talent it seems can still thrive in the Antipodes?'

'And unluckily Imogen has ended up in O'Rourke's college?'

'Recently I submitted an article to *The Sounds of Babel*, a journal run by a Leeds publishing house called Squibb's. It was rejected, although it's Editor – Professor Dick Summers in Boston – is a great enthusiast for the early Scandinavian languages ... '

'Did he see it?'

'Squibb's claimed he had, but O'Rourke, as head of the ethics committee – which rubber-stamps or rejects all research projects and articles – might have some leverage there.'

'So might have blocked it?'

Matthew gave a contorted grimace.

'Contact this Professor Summers and ask if he ever saw it?'

'Yes ... I could do that.'

He went over to his toy railway, where he pushed a

wagon along the track with a finger. Suddenly he looked a bit down, so I leapt up, turned him round and held his upper arms. 'Matthew, don't fold. We'll give this bunch a run for their money.'

He gave a tentative smile. 'I have an idea ... though it's a long shot.' The sun had broken through.

CHAPTER FIVE

The shepherd's hut in rural Northumberland, had been flattened and caterpillar-track marks showed that a mechanical digger had been busy all around it.

I flagged down a tractor.

The florid-faced farmer jumped down. 'Good morning young lady. So troublesome.' He waved a hand at his sizeable tractor. 'She's only firing on three cylinders.'

I nodded. 'Who levelled this hut?'

His face went blank. 'We wish we knew. It's uninhabited here ... but we think it happened at night.'

'Strange.'

'Very. Anyway, this morning I'm spreading lime on the Scorestone lower piece.'

'What does lime do?'

'It makes the soil less acid. This field's acidic despite being clayey. It should increase the grass yield.'

With a friendly wave he climbed back into his tractor and – towing its spreader – it lurched noisily off.

In The Tankerville Arms in Wooler, a little girl screamed, 'You howubble, howubble dog!' as she blubbered and nursed her rag-doll which had a severed right arm. A terrier lying nearby opened a guilty eye.

Over a T-bone steak, mash and cabbage, I pondered the extent of the excavation. Had the grid reference been inexact or had the treasure hunters been pre-empted ... or misled?

My blackberry pie and custard arrived. Eirig often called Ceinlys his 'sweetie pie'. She could not love him though, because her head was full of kapok. Lodes could not love him because her head was full of selfishness ... and she was not the right one anyway. And now he found it hard to trust a girl. Yet I loved him ... and it is the curse of womanhood that only by loving can she find happiness.

I drove to that upper track again. The harrow had disappeared as had my friend Mr Toro; so one less 'moosance'.

Thick herbage grew both in and around the derelict barn, which might have been muddled up with the shepherd's hut, but if this loot were not *under* the ground, where else might it be?

The coppice was of silver birch, though a lone fallen oak lay nearby, partly split and with its top charred, having been struck by lightning. In its hollow upper trunk I found only white mould and moss.

A soot-black cinder-like rock was not a meteorite I decided, just a lump of basalt.

I sat down in the long grass, drank tea and ate a foil-wrapped biscuit.

I imagined Eirig's blue-grey eyes and his drooping left lid. I smiled. He said I had a soft nature, not hard as with many girls. 'What is this love,' says the Song of Songs, 'that we abjure it not?'

A clump of sticky celandine swayed and a badger's snout appeared. We eyed one another and I waved gently, but it withdrew.

I groaned with exasperation. I ought to set off home, but was reluctant to give up the search. I felt that I was near.

The southern boundary of this wooded acre was a briar-entwined fence. I climbed a stile and – when on the rough public track – gazed at the grassy meadow opposite.

Then a feeble bleating sound caught my ear.

I pressed down the barbed wire and the pig-netting between two of the wooden posts and straddled the fence.

Again I heard this piteous whimper.

Between some tall mallow plants with their reddy-purple quinquefoil flowers and a boundary hedge lay a sheep on its side, terrified and trembling, ensnared in a coil of rusty wire which the farmer must have left after repairing the fence. I knelt down and patted it. 'I won't hurt you,' I whispered. Gently I unwound the wire from round its neck and a foreleg until – despite its unhelpful jerky movements – I eventually freed it. For twenty seconds it just stared and I thought it had given up its spirit and would die, until suddenly it sprang up and gambolled off.

My heart quivered. How silly, but I wept.

From the dense vegetation separating this field from the next, came a soft gurgling sound. I probed the brambles and thistles, until I glimpsed a tiny half-hidden beck trickling along in a shallow ditch before running into a cast-iron pipe, which took it under the track.

The word 'culvert' had been cited as a 'clue' in the note handed to Grieff; a word yielded up under torture perhaps?

I edged forwards through the tangled flora. Pink toadstools and floppy dock leaves were kind to my knees, but once in the beck's squelchy humus, it was sharp stones and soggy twigs. Traces of light filtered through the pipe from its far end.

Then I found what felt like a brick, a very heavy and slimy oblong brick. So was this it? Was this Aladdin's cave?

Had someone on the run, with not enough time to dig a proper pit, stowed his plunder in this strange hidey-hole?

I extricated myself with just three small bars of metal, each about the size of a thickish one-hundred-gram chocolate bar. My cagoule had been torn and my hands scratched by thorns.

I placed an old blanket on the driver's seat of my Polo and brushed my hands together before pulling on a pair of gloves to keep the Polo's controls clean.

In a deserted ox-bow lay-by on a back road near Alnwick, I washed my hands more thoroughly with an old sock and some screen-wash, before dumping my cagoule, gloves and wet trousers in a litter-bin and pulling on an old skirt and a spare pair of socks which lay on the back seat.

A van drew up. Its driver threw an empty crisp packet out of his window, then a milk carton.

I walked up to him. 'Hey Abanazar, there's a rubbish-bin over there.'

I received two fingers, then an apple-core which bounced off my chest.

Such an attitude signals the dissolution of a society more than say theft. The second at least has a logic to it. I picked up his litter.

A couple climbed a stile. They had been picking sloes from the edge of a wheat field. 'Early, this year,' hailed the man, 'and the blackberries are almost ripe too.'

In my hotel room in Jesmond, I ate pistachio nuts and thought of Jeremiah who had been denounced by the high priests, beaten and clamped in the stocks by the Upper Benjamin Gate. They had scoffed at him and called him a liar, yet though looked down on by the nobs and judges in Jerusalem, he knew that his words were true; and that God was with him.

I wallowed in a bath of soapy water and felt human once again.

I thought of the sheep I had saved. Sheep I knew had thirty-two teeth, eight of which were incisors in the lower jaw. The upper jaw had no incisors but a hard fibrous pad which with the opposing lower incisors tore up tufts of grass.

In bed, I quickly fell asleep.

*   *   *   *

My fair-to-blonde hair was bunched into its usual two stubby tufts and I wore a loose sage-green dress with a cord tie round its waist. Eirig wore an egg-yolk-dotted T-shirt and sun-faded long shorts. If not quite rustics come to market, we were not far off.

By contrast Lucinda – who was in her early forties – was tall, quite elegant and well-tended. Her dress was satin-like and slim-fitting, her hair nicely done up and her cheeks and eyelids had a little sparkly make-up on them. She greeted us with superficial warmth and led us through the kitchen to the patio which looked out onto her very pretty walled garden.

She introduced her boyfriend, Digby, a fellow of about thirty who 'wrote', was big on hair and eyed us with a hint of saturnine condescension.

'Sophie's from Harlech,' said Lucinda, correctly rasping the final consonants.

Digby cleared his throat.

I explained that I was a history researcher and that Eirig was a signalman on the railways, facts which were absorbed with mild curiosity, as of some rarely encountered species.

The coffee and apple-cake with cream, were first-rate.

'The apples are pulped Charles Ross ... from those trees trained along the wall there,' remarked Lucinda.

I nodded with genuine appreciation. 'So you enjoy baking?'

'Oh yes. One needs relief from academia.'

I mentioned the sculpture of Tanit in her hallway. 'My flat-mate in Newcastle learnt Phoenician.'

'Oh? The words "Punic" and "Phoenician" come from the Greek for "purple" because of the dye found in those famous molluscs off the Levantine coast.'

'Dusty says that you read theology as an undergraduate?'

'No. I put that on my UCAS form, but I'm not religious, so when I arrived, I swapped to politics and economics.'

'Oh.'

'I hear you've acted in a film Sophie ... *A Surfeit of Devils*?'

'Yes. Only a short one-scene part. I like acting ... but perhaps lack subtlety?'

'And it's a tough world. What parts do you prefer?'

'Any I think ... so long as they're credible.'

'Oh absolutely. I could never take the part of a white imperialist. I would rather die.'

I had not said that I minded being a bad lot, but did not argue the point.

'Are you and Eirig ... er ... together?'

'No, just cousins ... and friends,' said Eirig.

'His girlfriend's called Ceinlys,' I said.

Eirig sighed. 'I so love her.'

I think my cheeks dimpled.

Lucinda said that she and Digby hoped to marry in the spring.

'Oh, congratulations,' I said, whilst thinking that they deserved one another.

Eirig nodded. 'Women like commitment.'

Digby agreed. 'Even the ones you're not marrying do.'

I was unsure how to read this. Did he have other bits of fluff on the side?

'Finding the right partner can be difficult.' Lucinda glanced at me with sympathy.

'Matthew said that for one upper-crust student, it took her just ten minutes and two rum and Cokes.'

'Oh?'

'She met this guy and they "instantly clicked". He's a smuggler from Honduras.'

Eirig chalked up, 'An established stereotype; spoilt rich girl, bored, throws herself at some renegade.'

Lucinda demurred. 'Yes ... I would take Matthew's assertions with a pinch of salt.'

'If wealth is offered in exchange for love,' I said solemnly, 'it will be utterly scorned ... at least in secret if not openly.'

Lucinda and Digby appeared not to hear this.

'You're a professor in the politics faculty?' queried Eirig.

'Yes. An emeritus professor, a personal chair ... not head of department.'

She propounded the merit of all Europeans being fused together.

I wondered if she might do more good by working in a bakery.

'Yet still allowing them to "live as they wish",' she appended.

Eirig responded, 'That is certainly the prevailing drift, though it means that society will become less cohesive.'

'Which is why it must in parallel, adhere to a set of strict sociological tenets.'

I thought about this. 'Then won't life's pith and uniqueness be lost?'

'Our aim is to create concord ... not to promote petty tribalism.'

'Oh.'

Eirig summed it up. 'It sounds like a recipe for engineering robots.'

There was a period of silence.

Lucinda and Digby – like so many other 'intellectuals' – seemed more worried about how others might perceive their beliefs, than in giving thought to what they actually believed.

'I've met Imogen,' I confessed, switching I hoped to a less thorny topic. 'She shared with you, it seems, a strong wish to study in Oxford?'

'Yes ... she's quite a dry bone though, don't you think?'

'Umm ... she's restrained.'

'And quite religious?'

'She's reading Biblical Hebrew, but not theology as such.'

Digby rolled his eye-balls. 'Religion ... it treats us like sheep instead of intelligent beings.'

Eirig cogitated on this. 'The parable holds good though in one sense.'

'Does it?'

'Yes. We're all vulnerable – figuratively at least – to wolves, lions and untrustworthy shepherds.'

More coffee was poured.

'As to Imogen,' I back-tracked, 'she's quietly animated and free of gimmickry or pathos.'

Since this also evoked no reply, I intimated that I would like a second slice of apple-cake and a dollop of the clotted cream and Lucinda obliged.

Our hostess spoke of Imogen's 'A' level results. 'She gained a B in art, an E in French and a D in Italian. You normally need four grade A's and even then it's a tough haul to secure a place here.'

'That spells "bed",' put in Digby.

'Yes, but she won a scholarship,' I said. 'So they have to bend the rules?'

'Still, that degree of "bend" is ... highly unusual. The War-Zone Orphan and the Non-White Refugee bursaries say, are given *some* lee-way, but are not a complete walk in the park.'

Baffled, I repeated, 'Yet once tagged to the winner of this art competition ... they're bound, surely?'

'They could have reneged ... found some loop-hole.'

'In her gap year she spent six months on a kibbutz, then joined an archaeological dig ... before going to Strasbourg to this European art contest.'

Digby yawned loudly. 'Working in Israel should score negative points.'

'Why?' Eirig queried.

Lucinda looked at him with incredulity. 'It's called "shooting yourself in the foot".'

Eirig remained flummoxed.

'No, a scholarship, given to a *white* girl, from a *privileged* background ... she attended Malvern Saint James Girls' School ... is just shocking.'

I thought of poor Dusty, stuck with this pair.

Lucinda poured cream delicately onto the surface of her third cup of coffee off the back of her teaspoon, before stirring it.

'Tell us about Morocco,' I said cheerily.

She brightened up. 'When the *adhan* wailed from the minarets, no one took a blind bit of notice. Also I saw not one woman in a burka ... although some wore headscarfs.'

'That's encouraging,' I agreed. 'It seems that the degree of fanaticism varies markedly from one place to another in the Islamic world?'

'The women seemed pretty free too, the young men temperate if a bit boisterous ... and the French influence is still very evident ... courtesy, good manners.'

Digby parried this with, 'It'll be different in the mountain villages.'

'I daresay. Poor girls.'

For once, Lucinda and I were on the same side.

Détente was not Digby's strong point. 'Islam – as with socialism – owes its strength to the masses.'

'So *not* to individuals?' I asked. 'Is that good?'

'Yes.'

I baulked at this. 'So scrub out Shakespeare, Goethe, Handel, Solzhenitsyn, Ruth?'

Digby inspected his knife, then on reflection licked it. 'Who's Ruth?'

I had had enough of this wool-gathering and depressive

egoist. 'This was once a country of liberty, of eccentricity, of gentle humour.'

He sneered, 'And that means giving anyone asylum if they need it.'

I had not wanted this, but could not just silently acquiesce. 'If a brigand in a foreign country faces a draconian punishment for some crime, it's not our task to rescue him.'

'Well, that all depends upon your values, your humanity, doesn't it?' snapped Lucinda.

A hostile silence descended. The grit particles in the bottom of my coffee cup were, I decided, grounds for leaving.

We thanked our hostess for the lovely coffee and apple-cake and exchanged stock smiles.

After fifty yards, Eirig exhaled. 'What a delightful tea-party ... leg-pulls, jolly banter, croquet on the lawn, cheese and cucumber sandwiches?'

'If their opinions are rose-tinted, then ours I suppose are charcoal-tinted.'

'Do you think she'll throw you out of the flat?'

'Their every word almost is tendentious ... card players, scrabbling to win tricks.'

'Is your stuff safe?'

'I've a securely locked chest ... and the important stuff's at home.'

A soft crimson sun sank slowly over the roof-tops. I hoped he might take my hand.

Instead he said, 'Deep down, I think she's unhappy?'

'And angry. She's angry with us, angry with Digby, angry with almost everything ... but somehow keeps a lid on it.'

At the railway station, Eirig's train was late.

He hesitated. 'This ex-girlfriend of mine ... '

'Lodes?'

'I rang her a week ago in the middle of the night. Perhaps I shouldn't have?'

'How long were you together?'

'A year ... just over.'

'Such an impulse then is understandable ... but perhaps not at three in the morning?'

'She said if I did it again, she would report me to the police.'

As his train rumbled into the platform, we held one another's arms, kissed briefly on the lips, then parted company. I did not look back at him, which is said to be a sign of sincere affection. Only false lovers keep waving and throwing kisses.

*   *   *   *

Corporal Gorton's trial had dragged on for two months and run up astronomic legal fees.

On the stairs up to the public gallery, hung a picture of a stipendiary magistrate who had served in Oxford in the fifties. He had been a high court judge in India in the days of the Raj and had – the label said – on occasion handed down the death penalty.

Grieff was five-foot two, bald, something of an impresario and frequently witty at someone else's expense.

In the cafeteria a press reporter remarked to a colleague on Grieff's 'brilliance'. After choosing the dumplings, he expanded, 'Didn't understand a word mind you, but *utterly* brilliant.'

So 'utterly brilliant' in law equals 'conjuring up red herrings to confuse the jury'?

He had shown the court a ballistics graph. Its axes, $c + z^3$ and $\log 2a - x^2$ had some supposed link to muzzle velocity. No one I am sure, understood a word of it.

The soldier's former commanding officer had in the witness box also been skilfully blocked from making his point.

With my tea and bun, I sat down at his table.

'Colonel, may I ask a question?'

He raised an eyebrow.

I spoke softly. 'Has Mervyn Grieff ever been implicated with the handling of stolen platinum ... or silver?'

'Why do you ask?'

'Clues exists which suggest such.'

'Hmm ... unlikely. Why risk getting your hands dirty, when the lucre is pouring in anyway?'

'No, I see that.'

'These top lawyers know which side their bread's buttered on.'

'It seems to be buttered on both sides.'

He gave a short bitter laugh.

'As to this case, I understood that the Good Friday Agreement drew a line under older prosecutions?'

'So did we, but no, only the I.R.A. terrorists received an amnesty, not British soldiers.'

This was what my father would call, 'Another piece of smooth, disingenuous, Blairite politicking.'

'Thanks anyway.' About to stand up, he beckoned me

to sit down. I leant forward.

'In 2012, bars of precious metal from a bank in Galway were being taken to Belfast, but the convoy was ambushed just south of the border.'

'And this was platinum?'

'Some of it was ... and later a "prominent barrister" represented a Metropolitan police officer, who was believed to have shielded a fence.'

'By destroying evidence?'

He eyed me and nodded.

'Thank you.'

After lunch, the defence lawyer summed up his client's case in a quietly delivered masterpiece of factual brevity. The jurors were out for under forty minutes and the soldier was acquitted.

This defence barrister bowed politely to the bench, whilst Grieff – after we had all stood and the judge retired – left in a flurry perhaps to chew the carpet or to begin work on an appeal backed by legal aid and perhaps by some shadowy anti-military outfit.

Many in the court were well dressed and I suddenly felt a bit scruffy.

I went and bought a good quality tartan skirt, black and white – which is called 'shepherd's tartan' I believe – and a dark green woolly with a sheep knitted onto its front. Childish I know, but I do have that streak.

In the Queen Street public library, I learnt that the contraband mentioned by Colonel Grey, was thought to have sailed on a ferry from Larne to Cairnryan inside a six-wheeled tanker loaded with rape-seed oil. It consisted of eight bars of silver, four of platinum and five of gold. The far heavier gold ingots – each weighing four hundred troy ounces or *circa* twelve point four kilograms – represented the lion's share of the value.

On the ground floor of the Westgate Centre, an exhibition of contemporary African art was being held in an empty retail unit. Its organiser was a Dr Mpofu, whose name I recognised from the staff list of the Fine Arts Faculty.

A view of the veldt and another of a wooden and corrugated-iron mission church were unpretentious but not emotive. They were 'just pictures'.

A third, showing gazelles grazing around rusty railway tracks overgrown with grass and wild flowers had a lighter more buoyant feel and was signed, 'Luke Mpofu, 2020.'

Black, wiry and with a gleeful smile, he came over.

'Is "airy" the word?' I asked. 'It's more than just a scene ... it has atmosphere.'

'Thanks.'

He was Zimbabwean and had fled penniless from Mugabe's *régime* in 2001 to Kampala in Uganda, where he had worked in the Nalukolongo railway depot oiling diesel engines, until a series of bizarre events – which could have formed the plot of a Victorian novel – ended with his becoming a junior lecturer in fine arts, in Oxford.

'Do you paint?' he asked.

I smiled by squinting my eyes. 'At school I painted a woman whose arm bent in a gradual curve, instead of being angled at the elbow. The teacher asked me if she were made of plasticine?'

He gave a lively laugh.

'And my sun no doubt was the classic egg yolk with chips arranged radially around it?'

'What counts is your enjoyment ... and nowadays there is more interest in the process than the result.'

'How do you find the Department?' I probed.

'In the University? There are five of us, but we each have our own specialist patch ... so we don't interact much.'

I felt a more natural rapport with him than with most Indians or Arabs I had encountered. A sort of Freemasonry exists between those who are open and willing to just be themselves.

In the supermarket, in a deserted aisle, a familiar-looking figure came nervously towards me. It was the little man from the printers.

After glancing round, he said, 'The police have been and asked who had access to the image of that cheque.'

'Oh?'

'Only the finance manager and the pay girl are supposed to see that side of things.'

'Did they question you?'

'No.'

'Well if they do, say *nothing*. They'll start off very friendly, they'll want to be "helpful", to "make it easy for you", but if you once admit one tiny thing, you're doomed ... and so will I be.'

He gave a shuddering nod.

I repeated with emphasis, 'Say *nothing*. Nothing at all.'

It was Eirig's birthday, but he had to work in the signal-box at Ebbford.

I bought a bottle of non-alcoholic bubbly, two ham, gherkin and mustard rolls and two Danish pastries; studied a large-scale map and set off.

As I drove, I felt uneasy about that cheque. How could

anyone know that it had been copied?

I parked near a disused and weed-choked canal, climbed over a post-and-rail fence, passed a notice forbidding trespass on the railway and walked along in a gully parallel to the track.

A yellow distant signal up ahead moved from the horizontal to the lower quadrant position with a metallic clang. Then the cream and brown wooden cabin, raised up on a lower storey of Staffordshire blue engineering bricks came into view.

I climbed the steps and knocked. Eirig was truly overcome. He kissed me, then opened and stood my 'Happy birthday' card on the long wooden shelf with the dials and bells which ran at eye-level above the cast-iron levers.

'Quite small and cosy,' I observed.

'Only thirty-one levers. It's due to be closed soon and the signalling over the whole section controlled by one large electronic box.'

Ceinlys sat on the unlit iron stove.

I shook her fingerless hand. 'So you're his substitute girlfriend?'

'She tells me,' Eirig expounded, 'that she has no interest in morons with purple Lamborghinis.'

'Well that's a relief.' I looked at her. 'Sensible girl.'

'And we're particularly happy today because the neighbour's doll-destroyer's poorly.'

'Her dog?'

'Yes.'

On the shelf above the heavy red blue or black painted levers which moved the signals and the points, were various brass bells and bits of electrical equipment.

'This is a "three-position constant current telegraph". Inside is an electro-magnet. If the direct current flows towards the positive, the needle will be on the blue bit of the dial. If you reverse the current by depressing the knob, the needle will move to the red part and the change will also be replicated in the next box down the line. If there's a current failure, the needle will settle in the mid-position.'

'Oh?'

'The red means "train in block" and the blue "no train in block". A change also triggers a vibrating bell in the receiving box which its signalman will then cancel to acknowledge.'

'Hmm.' On top of the large wooden tool-box, I opened the bubbly and set the rolls out on paper napkins.

Ceinlys declined.

'She's watching her waist, aren't you my sweetie?'

'It looks thin enough.'

'In the evenings, she likes a card game. That's her chief bit of fun each day.'

'Oh. Which game do you play?'

'Solitaire.'

Whilst Eirig nipped out and into the trees for a wee, I whispered to Ceinlys, 'I'm a teensy bit envious of you.'

She just smiled.

I had put on my new skirt and woolly. Eirig was not at all clothes-conscious, but it is still right to try to endear yourself and give signs of respect to your beloved.

I had a flashback from the court. A Pakistani fellow had been handing out free fast-food vouchers to a group of young police officers who were also in the cafeteria, exchanging jokes and video-clips like school kids.

Next, Richard – the chap who worked in the printers – I, Stephanie and perhaps Roderick, should be the only ones who knew of that cheque being copied ... unless a second and independent source – someone say in Westminster, a chameleon, pink whilst in his Whitehall office, but blue when alone – had leaked it?

I sat on the old wooden chair and Eirig on the row of back-up accumulators. 'This equipment all looks pretty ancient?'

'Most of this was installed in the 1920s, but the technology's basically Victorian.'

I tried to recall Ohm's law: voltage equals current times resistance?

A phone message arrived from Lucinda giving me a week's notice to leave the flat. A 'close friend' needed it. 'The accommodation office have found a room for you in Newlove College's Tickell Lane Annex.'

We clinked our slightly dirt-ingrained mugs and imbibed. 'Happy birthday.'

'Thanks.'

'Is there a way of determining where a lump of say silver or platinum has come from?'

'If you mean, "Where was it mined?" then an analysis of trace elements – lead, antimony, tin, bismuth, say – would pin-point that ... but you would need a metallurgy lab to do it.'

We each took a roll and munched.

'Why the curiosity?'

'It's to do with a court case going on in Oxford.'

'If the platinum came from the Urals – for instance –

that would still be demonstrable even if an ingot were recast. Is it stolen?'

'Yes.'

'Haven't the lawyers had it analysed?'

'I don't think they know where it is? Still, never mind. I'll await developments.'

All the electrical devices on the shelf were duplicated, one set for the neighbouring box in each direction.

There was a simple code for ringing a warning bell in the next box: one acknowledge, two passenger train, three goods train, four light engine, five obstruction. Eirig hit three bells for the next box up the line and moved two levers forwards.

'I'm flattered that you've come to see me.'

'I should be hacked off if you weren't.' I tilted my brows inwards, but though amicable, the atmosphere was not romantic.

A goods train approached. The box shook and then came the regular beat of the wagon wheels as they clunked over the joints in the track.

Eirig's relief arrived and we drove to his top-floor flat in Stroud in our separate cars.

He heated up two ready meals, but burnt them.

'Carbon is good for cleansing impurities out of your gut.'

'And this brown seaweed will be rich in something, no doubt?'

'It's cabbage'

We binned the meals, ate cake, drank wine and played cards.

Eirig had two kings, two queens and a knave. 'I've never been into a real court.'

'Well in law courts there are no kings or queens, but plenty of knaves.'

'Deuce floats.'

'Does it?' I hoped we would float ... or at least have a tussle and a tickle.

'Deuce is two.'

'Today, one clever witness named a double-murder committed by one of the plaintiffs. This historical act should not have been disclosed, so the judge silenced him and instructed the jury to ignore it.'

'Yet the seed had been sown?'

'Yes and every quibble or request for an adjournment from the prosecution he had apparently upheld.'

'Law has little to do with right or wrong.'

I quoted, '"Clever speech is the brandy of the damned."'

'Let's have a game of Scrabble? But ... we'll only use *regular* English words?'

'Unless I'm losing ... then prepare for "kicks" spelt "QYKZ".'

I lost but happily so.

As I left, we exchanged our customary quick kiss on the lips, then looked whimsically at one another. I sensed he wanted to go farther but was frightened.

I smiled benevolently.

Hesitatingly, he took hold of me. 'I've wanted to do this before, but I wasn't sure.'

We nuzzled one another. 'You great silly,' I cried.

*   *   *   *

With my blue umbrella patterned with red dots, I battled the gusts and the rain squalls as I crossed the car park at the motorway services.

I placed my fish, chips and peas and a glass of phosphorescent bubbly lime juice on a table in a quiet recess.

Stephanie joined me.

'The fish is dry and white and the batter thin; no baking powder in it.' I looked at her. 'Any come-back about that account tracing?'

Stephanie gave a faint smile. 'One day we shall retire and life will be good.'

I salted my chips. 'And in the meantime?'

My boss took a fish-bone from between her teeth. 'Sophie, I'm going to tell you something. I'm worried.'

I met her eye.

'That cheque ... I've done something else ... something even more stupid.'

'Oh?'

'What happened to Judith upset me, so I sent a copy of it to two national newspapers together with an explanation of what it had paid for.'

'The police have been to the printers in Howe Street.'

'Neither paper ran the story ... but one must have tipped off some government agency.'

'But you did it anonymously? So they can't track it to you?'

'Not definitely, but if they logged that account search and then spotted Judith's stabbing and saw that her married name is "Norman" – even though she sticks with "Amos" for her University work – they might be tempted to "deduce"?'

'Hmm.' I breathed deeply.

'I've heard of this sort of thing before ... and believe me, they'll leave no stone unturned. They're utterly ruthless.'

'If they do suspect you, what might they do?'

'I don't know.'

'That Richard guy's scared stiff and I stressed to him – very strongly – to say absolutely nothing.'

'Good.'

'A dessert?'

'Er ... the tangerine cheese-cake, please.'

When I returned, I said, 'They might try to trick you ... use a friendly journalist ... had a tip-off, is hunting for a story?'

'I wouldn't fall for that.'

'My dad was in the Army and in the infantry a section is ten men; nine riflemen and one with a light machine-gun. The private with the Bren gun and one rifleman – who carries extra ammunition for the Bren – form the "gun group".

There are a set of commands known as "the section attack". The opening premiss is that you have come under "effective enemy fire" and the key word is "effective", because your enemy might just fire off a few random shots at night to see if you respond, so giving away your position.'

'So you do nothing?'

'Correct.'

'What happens if the enemy fire *is* effective? Clumps of earth start springing up around you?'

'Then the "gun group" gives covering fire whilst the other eight riflemen execute an encircling movement to take out the enemy from behind ... and the final command in this "section attack" sequence is "reload", the reason being that – having taken the redoubt – you might then have to repel a counter-attack.'

'Hmm ... a sort of parallel to my predicament.' She took her last bite of cheese-cake.

'Stephanie, liberty requires courage. I don't see anything wrong with what you did. At least we're being brave even if others are scared.'

She dabbed her lips. 'My grandfather was a *Lysander* pilot for a period during the war ... taking agents into and out of France ... a real-life *Biggles*.'

'Gavin O'Rourke's been interviewed on local television – together with Syed Husaini from *The Grasshopper* – discussing Oxford's future.'

She nodded soberly. 'Yes, he's the linch-pin or spear-head in culling anyone who dissents from the new *status quo*."

'The puppeteer behind the scenery.'

'The tag "diversity and equality" has always struck me as absurd. They're opposites.'

'You're thinking too much. Coffee?'

'Yes ... er, it's my turn.'

When she returned with the coffees and a small bar of chocolate, I asked, 'On the "reload" topic, can I tell you a story?'

'I'm listening.'

'A corporal on patrol in Jerusalem in forty-seven, saw an Arab toss a grenade into a café used by Europeans. He unshouldered his Sterling, fired a couple of shots, but missed. He chased the fellow who then climbed up onto a roof. The corporal climbed onto the roof too and they exchanged more shots, but again neither scored any hits.

The Arab then jumped down into a suq and vanished into the crowd. Later that day, walking down a quieter street, the corporal turned into an alleyway and found himself face to face with this fellow. Now to swing a sub-machine-gun on its webbing strap off your shoulder takes ... two seconds? The Arab had his pistol in his belt and so beat him to the draw, but when he pulled the trigger it just went "click". So remember, reload.'

Stephanie thought for a while. 'Sophie – on the topic of pistols – I want you to keep something for me.'

'Oh?'

'My pistol. It normally lives up the chimney in its box, wrapped in plastic ... there's a ledge there where a brick's missing.'

'Why are you giving it to me?'

'I'm frightened that I might use it.'

'What? Take your life?'

'No, no. I would never do that. I'm worried that if threatened ... well ... I would rather suffer wrongly than kill someone.' She had read classics at Cambridge. 'Socrates said, "It is better to suffer a wrong that to commit a wrong."'

'Oh.'

'Do you have anywhere to hide it?'

'Er ... I think it would go under our garden shed ... and there're plenty of weeds and dirt there to keep it company.'

'The coffee's good for a change.'

'Small delights.'

We walked out to the car park where the rain had stopped and the sun glinted off the puddles.

She opened the boot of her car and gave me a package.

*   *   *   *

Sited some way from the city centre, Newlove was one of the newer Oxford colleges and also the one where Imogen was enrolled. I went there to collect my keys for the Tickell Lane Annex.

A notice pinned up in the foyer by one Helena Tremayne sought to form a college netball team.

In this Annex – a converted Victorian mansion with thirteen single study-bedrooms – I settled in to my new first-floor abode.

A home-made sign in the hallway read, 'Please be quiet during the day-time. The students are trying to sleep.'

A poster headed 'The Isis Dramatic Society' gave the audition dates for their forthcoming autumn-term play, an English translation of Aeschylus's *The Eumenides*. Producer Carole Grieff. Application forms available in the Students' Union or from the secretary, Alison Hayball.

Whilst sticking a label onto my mail-box, I recognised two names; Emma Hyman and Alison Hayball.

In the upstairs kitchen, a girl stood stirring some lentil, onion and tomato concoction with chunks of salami and bay leaves in it.

'Hullo. I'm Sophie.'

'Hi. Alison. Alison Hayball.'

After fighting a roll of paper towels which refused to tear along its pretend perforations, she asked if I would like a bowl of her recipe?

'That's very kind. It smells lovely.'

She placed a second spoon on the table.

'I see Emma Hyman lives here.'

'Yes. She's the sub-warden ... being a post-grad. She has the old drawing-room ... the only one with a bedroom partitioned off.'

The stew was surprisingly tasty.

It being the summer holidays, it was very quiet. 'Who else is in residence at the moment?'

'I think Libby's in, though she tends to stay in her room, meditating with her crystals.'

'Oh. What do you study?'

'Botany ... but I spend a lot of my time with amateur music groups.'

'Do you know of a Judith Amos?'

'Yes. She gave us some lectures in my first year. She's quite renowned for her Ph.D.'

'Oh?'

'She proved a mathematical theorem, which no one had previously managed to demonstrate. Two and a half pages.'

'Two and a half pages? So succinct ... and done in an afternoon perhaps?'

'She's just had an article on the mineral content of vegetables blocked though.'

'Blocked?'

'By the ethics committee.'

'Oh. Can scientific experiments have ethical dimensions?'

'Oh yes. If laboratory animals might suffer ... or if there's something unfashionable in it ... about climate change say?'

'Unfashionable?'

'Yes. Politics plays a large part in everything now.'

I asked about the auditions for *The Eumenides*.

'They're in four weeks. The Society puts on a play at the end of each term ... subsidised by the arts committee.'

'I quite like acting.'

'It'll be *very* competitive.'

'Oh.'

'It's easier just to join an *ad hoc* group. To put something on in the quad, all you need is permission from the warden or the bursar.'

'Could I have a form, none the less?'

'Yes of course.'

'Why are the auditions so early?'

'The leads need to learn their lines before rehearsals start ... so if a student wants a part, he or she just has to come up.'

I opened the cupboard with the name 'Anne' on it. A half-used packet of cereal stood there.

'Anne was a mature student – late twenties – reading French, but was also ... what are those part-time police officers called?'

'Special constables?'

'That's it. I think she did eight or ten hours a week ... but she was jeered at and called names ... It's so wrong. She's still a person, but all they see is the uniform.'

'I know.'

'I think she was a bit hacked off with policing anyway ... it was mostly "censorship" visits to people who had said something which had upset someone else.'

I made tea for us and luckily had some chocolate biscuits. 'This Carole Grieff, is she married to a top-level barrister?'

'Yes ... well at least they live in the same house.'

'Do you mean they don't get on?'

'It's only rumour. They live in a Jacobean mansion – Cotswold stone, Grade One listed – in Moreton-in-the-Marsh.'

I nodded. 'What's she like?'

'She's in the Classics' Department at Saint John's. Quite brusque, sharp ... energetic.'

'She beckoned me into her room to give me a form. 'Pop it under my door when you've completed it.'

A bassoon lay on the bed together with a score for a blues song, *Only Blue Stars Twinkle*, marked *con brio*.

As Alison had to catch a train, I offered to do the washing-up, then went out too, to buy a copy of *The Eumenides* which I later started to read, sitting cross-legged on my bed.

Next morning, in Exeter College, a fellow in a gown courteously held a door open for me, but a scruffy student, eyes fixed on the ground, elbowed me to one side and ambled through ahead of me, only to be waylaid.

'North, do you think I'm holding this door open for your miserable carcass to crawl through it?'

'Er ... sorry Sir.'

I gave a nod of thanks and passed through, only to be stopped by a black female hill-billy with bulging eyes and a 'BLM' T-shirt. The don and the student had now disappeared. 'Don't you think it sexist for him to hold a door open for you?'

'Er ... '

'You should be offended.' There was aggression in her tone.

She jabbed my shoulder with a bony index finger and thrust her face into mine. 'I hate white people,' she snarled.

I recoiled, which – by her glare I realised – infuriated her even more.

I discovered later that she was Professor Opoku and was well-known for both for her 'attitude' and for prodding anyone who annoyed her.

Matthew read of the flint glasses for the signal lamps on the N. and N.S.R. which as well as tin, had a trace of gold in them, giving a sparkling brilliant red.

'This book will be a hardback with sixteen full colour-plates and maps.'

'No spoiling the ship for a ha'p'orth of tar?'

We spent two hours deciding on the basic layout of the book, after which Matthew said, 'Let's have an early light lunch?'

At *The King's Arms* we chose the soup of the day, pea and ham.

'Lucinda's thrown me out of the flat.'

'Oh ... well I hope she receives a come-uppance.'

'It's called Digby. She must have lost her marbles.'

'Did Lord Elgin take them?'

The soup arrived.

'As a teenager she was quite savvy ... before she bought into this equality tripe.'

'In Osaka I and my sister went to a very old restaurant. All were dressed in colourful traditional costumes and behaved with a strictly prescribed decorum. We had barely come through the door when the head-waiter came up to us and apologised that foreigners were not admitted. He was courteous and recommended somewhere he thought we would find congenial.'

Matthew refilled our glasses with the *rosé*. 'If he did

that here, he'd be arrested.'

I fetched two fruit salads and a jug of cream.

'Shifting to Imogen, can you tell me about this Strasbourg art competition?'

'Yes. Although her ability to paint outstrips almost anyone, she lacks the creativity to design a good – or at least a complex – canvas. She paid for permission to sit in *La Galleria Nazionale d'Arte Antica* in Rome with her easel and brushes, to copy the self-portrait by Artemisia Gentileschi in which the artist herself is engaged in painting. It dates from 1638 when Artemisia was in England at the invitation of Charles the First. The unusual side-on view of the subject defines it as Baroque rather than Renaissance, as does the brighter centre and the plainer darker periphery.'

Our empty dishes were taken away.

'The judges were split. Her copy of this self-portrait was so flawless in texture and style – even invoking perhaps a life-like intensity greater than the original – that they had to admire her gift, but the lack of originality weighed against her. None the less, she won the prize; twenty-five thousand euros.'

'And the kudos ... and the scholarship here in Oxford?'

'And it cleared her debts. She had taken quite a gamble.'

I smiled. 'A simple but good lunch. Thank you.'

CHAPTER SIX

In Gloucester, I parked in a side-street with no surveillance cameras. Again I put on the pair of cracked sun-glasses and knotted a large burnt-orange headscarf under my chin.

My oblong bar of silver was a little over four inches by two, its thickness about half an inch. It had rounded corners and on its front were embossed the Royal Mint's coat of arms, 1000 g, 999 – which was its purity in parts per thousand – and a long serial number prefixed with an 'R'.

At the bottom of Westgate stood a drab narrow-fronted shop which advertised itself – in gold letters on peeling black paint – as a jeweller's. It was owned by one Laban Abrams, who had twice been arrested for acting as a fence, charged with melting down precious metal ingots and turning them into rings, tie-pins and such, but had yet to be successfully convicted.

In the window were antique brooches, rings, old coins and a wasp.

The brass bell above the door tinkled.

A spare elderly fellow with a straggly greying beard tottered in from a back-room. He could have been a fakir except for his gold-rimmed half-moon glasses and the woolly waist-coat on top of his long unwashed white shirt.

He gave me a thin, circumspect smile. 'Yeth Mith?'

I produced my bar of silver and placed it on the square pink velvet pad atop his diminutive counter. 'Can you make me an offer for this?' I knew its value to be somewhere between six and seven hundred pounds.

He stared at me for a long time.

'I'm not police or government.'

Again he eyed me carefully before drawing in the air with a forefinger the numbers 'three, nought, nought'.

I nodded and six fifty-pound notes were counted out.

A plaque on the wall read; 'The Lord our God, the Lord is one.'

I departed from the city unostentatiously and stopped in an empty lay-by to dump the headscarf and sun-glasses in a bin and to change my sister's cobalt blue jacket for my own dark green one.

I had prepared an envelope addressed to the chief executive at the head office of The Ulster Bank in Belfast. I had used newly purchased stationery and worn gloves. With a stencil template I had written a letter. Headed, 'The 11th. of August, 2020,' it said that the enclosed money had been given by a fence for the sale of one of their missing silver ingots and an accompanying photograph showed it with its serial number.

*   *   *   *

Imogen seemed quite happy that I should call.

'And bring a pizza?'

'All right.'

The painting on the easel had come a long way. Ruth was gleaning the stalks left behind by the reapers which still had ears on them.

The scene was calm and free of those allegorical allusions so beloved by the critics. Buff hills and ochre fields formed the background under a pale blue-grey sky. Ruth wore a calf-length faded blue dress with flecks of magenta around its hem and neck-line, the only dabs of a stronger colour. It had a sort of misty yet ordinary brightness about it. It was just so lovely.

'Your Uncle Matthew has a very water-damaged painting of the railway he's researching. It's beyond restoration, but could you make a copy of it?'

'Bring it round and I'll have a look.'

She led me into her bedroom to show me another of her paintings.

'It's a ruined watch-tower near Edom.'

Beside the dry dusty road which runs from Judaea down to the Dead Sea, it stood abandoned, crumbling. A screech owl sat on its battlements and yellow flowers sprouted from the cracks in its masonry. Overhead the sun blazed down on the arid plateau with its sparse thorn bushes and tufts of salt grass, whilst a jackal loped by in the distance, yet beneath this sand-scoured wilderness, you could sense life just surviving under the surface.

If viewed closely, her brush-strokes were a little om the rough side. Also she never used those contemporary colour-block methods, which although they can give an effective or an attractive result, are often I suspect a way of escape for those who cannot properly capture a face, an emotion or an ambience.

'Are you the top of your class?'

She bent over and laughed.

'Last term we had a one-hour assignment. We had to paint a space-ship with a kitchen implement. I hoped I might be given the pastry brush but ended up with the bread-saw. My effort was given a C minus ... bottom of the class.'

'How many little green men did you include?'

'Three.'

We cut up the pizza and poured grapefruit juice into glasses.

'A girl in Newlove is trying to scrape together a netball team. How about we join? You need some exercise?'

She acknowledged the truth of this. 'How many does she need?'

'Seven for a team ... plus a couple of reserves?'

'All right, but I can't play for toffee.'

'We're not aiming at the Olympics; just a bit of exercise.'

She grinned. 'Touch your toes.'

I did so, easily and lithely. 'Supple? Lissom? I had a book once, *Beginning Ballet*. It showed you the five positions for the feet, then *plies*, *petits battements* and so on.

Also, do you need a holiday?'

'Er ... I'd like one ... but I'm a bit hard up ... well perhaps enough for a few days in The Lakes?'

'It's too crowded there at this time of year.'

'Yes.'

Two flash cards bore obscure Moabitic words.

'The Vice-Chancellor asked about them.'

'The Vice-Chancellor?'

'He'd told Prof that he intended to visit with some Arts Council bigwigs, but the Prof forgot to tell his secretary or she would have put it in the diary.'

I smiled in anticipation.

'The Prof was away that day and the rest of the staff had gone to lunch when this cohort appeared. After a search they found a cleaner and then me. They referred to Prof as the holder of "The Mary Celeste chair of Fine Arts".'

'So lacking an alternative, they quizzed you about these cards?'

'Yes. Then went off to dine.'

We shared the last two slices of pizza.

'If next term, you're bothered again by other students, can I do anything?'

Imogen gave a constrained smile. 'It's two from fine arts, plus some of those feckless social science morons.'

I looked at her.

'I'll be all right.'

I think she feared that I might launch myself into a scrap. Her refusal to physically retaliate was more edifying, I have to concede, yet bullies – if you stand up to them – go off in search of easier prey.

As Imogen made coffee, I said, 'Lucinda's thrown me out.'

'Oh?' She paused. 'Actually I feel a bit sorry for her.'

Certainly that Digby's incapable of love ... at least of the emotional kind. He's a cloud with the wrong sort of silver lining.'

Imogen tried not to smile. 'She's a soul adrift.'

We sat on the sofa and I helped myself to a chocolate.

'Also Matthew's received a summons to a hearing. It bears a date and an address, but no name, no signature.'

I listened.

'It begins with a "summery", spelt with an "e".'

'Nought out of ten.'

'Allegations have been "bought" against him.'

'Still nought out of ten.'

'Unless they paid the accuser?'

'He should tell them to try selling pegs.'

'I know ... and this is supposedly a "top" university.'

'How serious is it?'

'He says he has an ace up his sleeve, but I wonder if wishful thinking is persuading him to over-value this unnamed card?'

'Is it regarding a book titled *Empire*, which someone placed in his pigeon-hole to stir up trouble?'

'No. It's a girl ... '

'Has he written a silly letter?'

'No. Touch ... allegedly.'

'Any witnesses?'

'No.'

'So probably concocted?'

She sort of smiled. 'Aren't they just shockers?'

'Did they say he was "viscous"?'

'Give them time ... and they'll get round to it.'

As I pulled on my jacket, I said, 'I'm glad I've come to Oxford and met you all ... I really am ... and yet I'm starting to wish for something ... away from the big city.'

'Hmm. Country life sounds appealing ... but that will be tough too ... in other ways.'

'No doubt.' I laughed. 'Good night.'

*   *   *   *

As I walked back into town, I saw Judith coming towards me.

'Ten past ten. Are you a night owl?' she asked.

In her house, she made cocoa.

'Alison, a girl in the college annex where I now live, says you've had scientific articles rejected on questionable grounds?'

'Well ... I determined the mineral content of various vegetables and they varied widely from those published by the Germans a long way back. For instance spinach has no iron in it. My Ph.D. student quipped that Popeye should have eaten the tins.'

'This sounds like critical stuff given diets, food labelling and such?'

'Yes, but other researchers have since based three hundred or more articles on the German work, so the big cheeses in the game don't want the boat rocked.'

'Is it a "gaggle" of ostriches?'

'Another one, not in any way controversial, about iron-eroding deep-sea bacteria, I thought original enough to be accepted ... but they can only publish a small percentage of the submissions they receive.'

I recalled images of the *Titanic* slowly decaying on the ocean floor.

'This bacteria article, to which journals did you send it?'

'Only one. *The Unicellular World.*'

'Is that owned or managed by Squibb's?'

'Er ... that rings a bell.' She sipped her drink. 'Will you keep a secret?'

'Yes.'

'I'm very worried about Stephanie. She says someone's been into her house.'

'Oh? How does she know?'

'She leaves certain books in very exact positions ... and they've been moved.'

'Hmm,' I growled throatily.

A small green linen flag lay on a chair. I pointed to it.

'It came in the post yesterday. We sometimes have threatening letters too.'

I nodded deeply.

'We haven't yet had a brick through the window, but I'm almost expecting it.'

'These people have no integrity.'

I finished my cocoa and left.

*　　*　　*　　*

I lay awake and thought of Stephanie. Without doubt, dark forces were gathering.

I thought of her pistol.

In 2015 six of us had spent a day on the ranges at Otterburn Camp, being shown how to fire and clean the Browning nine millimetre pistol. We had been taught the traditional firing position; sideways on to the target, feet slightly apart, left hand in the small of the back, right arm crooked at the elbow, left eye closed and right eye looking along the sights. Now, in films at least, you only see the two-handed semi-squatting position.

The plywood targets were five yards away. 'It's not a rifle,' Sergeant Davy had said. 'You're not going to hit someone beyond a few yards, regardless of what happens in Hollywood.'

Although the magazine was designed to hold thirteen rounds, it was advised not to insert more than ten, because if the spring is depressed too much too often, it loses its springiness. The short parabola-nosed bullets were also used in the Sterling sub-machine-gun.

I do not know if the Browning was ever issued with

a silencer. If it was, it was not mentioned. The velocity of a pistol bullet is sub-sonic. The crack comes from the expansion of the escaping gases after the bullet has left the barrel. I suppose a plastic fizzy drinks bottle with the bottom cut off would act like a car's exhaust silencer and dampen the shock wave, though it would be very clumsy. Perhaps just use a cushion?

After a long session, we went to the canteen. 'You can't miss it,' said the training major, 'it's the only building that's camouflaged.'

We sat down at a long table with some squaddies. They were rough, jovial, yet had a knack of saying simply and pithily what they felt about things, unlike the egg-shell-treaders of Oxford, ever fearful of being judged 'far right'.

I drove home.

With one of Dad's files, I filed the number off Stephanie's pistol. I punched holes in the flat green tin which held the cleaning kit and at a lonely spot on the River Dovey, threw them into the middle of the stream, followed by the twenty-two bullets. The unlabelled wooden box I dropped into a builders' skip.

*   *   *   *

In wondering how I might help Stephanie, I came up with a plan. I would make it appear that others must be disseminating STUB's secrets.

In *The Brewhaha*, Richard came in for his lunch at twelve-thirty.

Despite my new sun-glasses, he recognised me. I gave him the tiniest nod and after buying a pork and stuffing roll and a mug of tea, he joined me in an alcove, spilling a little tea onto the plastic table-cloth as he did so.

I tapped my crossword whilst whispering with barely any lip movement, 'Would you be able to get hold of data on other print jobs done for STUB's?'

He pretended he had nor heard, but I knew he had.

After twenty seconds and after biting a piece off his roll, he murmured, 'We've printed six or seven posters, but our main works near Brighton does the pamphlets.'

'Monopolise pig; three letters?'

'I'm the acting manager on Saturday ... so probably I could print off all the tenders, contracts and invoices linked to STUB's.'

This sounded good. 'Ah, "hog".' I filled in the clue.

Rather timidly he breathed, 'I've never been to America.' Then with a fine spray of crumbs added, 'Can you pay me?'

'A painter, Prometheus and I; six letters?' I mumbled. 'I think so.' I remembered my two platinum bars. 'Five thousand?'

'Yes, that would be sufficient.'

'Then shall we do it?'

He lowered his head minimally – half the thickness of a guinea-pig's prick as Dad would say – but it meant, 'Yes.'

'Prometheus was a Titan? So ... "Titian"?'

'The top of the Saxon Tower, Sunday, midday?'

As he left, I filled in my clue.

The next day, a Friday, I was back in Gloucester.

I strolled past Laban Abrams' shop and then back as I waited for a customer to leave.

He appeared to have sold the wasp. The bell tinkled

and despite my changed attire, he recognised me.

The platinum bar made his eyes widen. After another long look at me, he came round the counter, locked the door and turned the 'open' sign to 'closed'.

He led me through into a cramped and cluttered back room and opened an ancient but very solid looking safe. Its steel door was five inches thick. He took out a shallow wooden tray with thin plywood dividers and found room for it on the table by pushing a number of sauce and milk bottles to one side.

He waved at the money. 'In whole thousands, I have six.'

This was about a quarter of the value of the bar of platinum. The notes were all used ones.

I eyed him archly. 'I accept.'

*   *   *   *

We stood alone on the leaded roof of The Saxon Tower and gazed over the parapet towards the thin fretted spire of All Saints' Church.

A glint of happiness shone in Richard's left eye as we swapped my draw-string canvas bag for his knobbly A4 envelope.

'I scooped the pond. Everything's there.' He spoke huskily but with satisfaction.

'Excellent,' I nodded. 'The five thousand pounds is all in used twenties. You must *not* though put them through your own bank account.'

'Umm ... I can't pay for such a holiday in cash?'

'You could buy the dollars with cash.'

He scratched his chin. 'Dad's a widower with early dementia ... and a more or less dormant second bank account. The flight money could go through that.'

We shook hands.

I left first, passing on my descent the cell door from the old Bocardo Prison, behind which Thomas Cranmer had been imprisoned.

My contraband showed that N.I.S. and its sister company in Hove had, since the start of the year, completed twenty-eight print jobs for STUB UK. Six of these had been paid for from a Luxembourg account, four from one in Brussels and eighteen from their Bank of England account.

Via the internet I traced nine of the pamphlets paid for from the latter and printed them off. Their subjects varied, but were generally pro-European, anti-American and intended to undermine the white working class.

Later I posted nine anonymous letters to various newspapers and journals, each of which included one pamphlet with its invoice, payment slips and receipts; enough to substantiate the financial side of its production.

I put my spare printed copies in a file under the carpet under the bed in my room, went for a late run and then took a shower.

If Stephanie were being watched, they would know that these letters had not been posted by her.

*　　*　　*　　*

Libby had promised to lend me a book, a biography of the life of Zeno of Kition, the founder of Stoicism.

'It makes conjectures about his earlier follies and blind

spots, before speculating on how gradually life's reverses and experiences led him to his philosophy.'

'That,' I said encouragingly, 'sounds preferable to some ridiculous super-hero nonsense.'

Eleven o'clock struck from a nearby church and thinking to settle myself down and read the first chapter, I made a last cup of tea and then went to the window of my room, where a three-quarter moon hung above the roof-tops and a moderate wind blew. The tall overgrown buddleias swayed back and forth.

No sooner had I closed the curtains, than gravel rattled on the glass. I opened the curtains again and peered down. Stephanie stood there. I slid up the sash-window.

'Let me in,' she called softly.

I went down to the main door and did so. No one else was about.

My little room had a slightly sloping floor, a few patterned cushions and throws and two posters stuck on one wall. I was becoming fond of it.

Stephanie sat on the bed whilst I went to make her a cup of tea and toast some crumpets.

With music playing softly and our heads close together, she said, 'Someone's been into my house. I've been leaving doors and books in fixed positions so that I can tell if they've been disturbed ... and I've received a very menacing letter.'

'Might you have been followed here?'

'I checked my car as well as I could for trackers and I've left it near Judith's house ... so I don't think so.' She handed me a copy of the letter.

A high-ranking civil servant in the Ministry of Justice in

Petty France in London had written saying that they had received information that Stephanie had been a party to attempts to accuse Her Majesty's Government of bias by supporting various political campaigns and that if further evidence of such activity came to light, she would face suspension and investigation.

'Have you told Roderick about this?'

'No. There seems to be no point.'

'I think he ought to know ... in case anything more happens.'

'This will have been triggered by one of those two newspapers I sent stuff to.'

I thought for a time. 'They can only be guessing. This letter's only a bluff. Why not write back denying it and telling him to produce evidence rather than trying to pull rank ... after all, they're supposed to be lawyers?'

I could see that she was unsure.

I hesitated, but decided that I had to tell her about Richard and my new flurry of accusatory letters. 'I had intended it to divert attention from you, but ... '

'So now they certainly won't let it lie.'

I asked her to check for vehicles registered to the name of anyone named Jason Q. Lacey. There was one; in Harrogate; a Mercedes Smart 2003 Roadster, red and black. Number 103 JQL. I wrote down its details.

Outside we exchanged good-byes. I watched and waited for a time, then walked slowly along Tickell Lane, nipped deftly into a garden and hid. From there I kept watch for another twenty minutes. All seemed quiet.

CHAPTER SEVEN

The only way forward seemed to be to take more risks and Matthew had sown the seed of this next adventure.

Narrow Boat House stood opposite Granary Wharf on the Leeds to Liverpool Canal. I eyed this bland three-storey office block over the gaudily decorated barges.

The collator and design editor of the periodical *The Sounds of Babel* was a Jason Q. Lacey, its editor Professor Summers in Boston and its three sub-editors, academics in Edinburgh, Vienna and Auckland.

Squibb's Academic Publishing had its offices on the top floor.

I booked into the Doubletree Hotel and asked for a room facing the canal.

The receptionist obliged. 'One fifth-floor room is free. From there you can watch the boats.'

'Good. Thank you.'

'Oh cash? Do you have some form of I.D.?'

I showed him my second driving licence.

'Thank you.' He handed me my pass-card. 'Enjoy your stay Miss Owens.'

From my room I could look across at Canal Wharf and see a half of Narrow Boat House set back behind its car park.

At seven I went out to the nearby *Café Violette* and ordered a chicken breast with cheese sauce, chips and broccoli. I wore a plain skirt and a loose pullover.

There were few patrons, but a jittery, tanned young fellow came across and sat at my table.

'Hi there. Mind if I join you?'

'No.'

'I'm Abid ... from the Lebanon.'

'Oh.'

'Do you want a drink?'

'I have one thanks. I've not been to the Lebanon. Are you just visiting Leeds?'

'I'm an asylum seeker.'

'Oh. Waiting for your case to be heard?'

'Well ... that's on hold because I have back trouble.'

It struck me that he had walked easily enough.

His knee touched mine under the table so I withdrew mine promptly.

'Back pain is very hard to prove or disprove.' He gave me a sly wink.

'Yes, I can imagine.'

'I do have a bit – I used to work loading ships – but my lawyer explained how to exaggerate it ... how do you say ... without overdoing it?'

'Did he?'

'There's talk of an operation to remove the disc which has been squeezed out into the spinal canal and is chafing the nerves ... but my lawyer says not to admit to any improvement.'

'So your case still wouldn't be heard?'

'Exactly.' He grinned and clearly expected me to approve.

I slurped my drink and took another bite of chicken.

'Do you want to spend the night with me?'

'No,' I said brusquely.

He smiled and stood up. 'Oh well, see you around.'

'Happy Christmas,' I muttered.

He headed off to a hefty girl sat at the bar. She had short cowboy-style tooled black boots and a very short mini-skirt. In between these lay an expanse of blotchy tattooed coarse-looking flesh; two lumpy bare thighs. Abid might have more luck there, I thought.

The television beside the bar was showing a cartoon. A prisoner loaded a cannon, but in error put the ball from his own ball and chain into the barrel, so when the cannoneer lit the fuse, he was hurled across the sky by the fired ball shackled to his ankle.

Could this be me tomorrow?

I was starting to feel nervous, like the night before your first parachute jump.

In my room I drank a miniature Cointreau and a coffee, ate chocolate and – to cheer myself up – tried to imagine Imogen's bread-saw-created Martians. I made up a ditty.

A Martian space-ship landed near
The Royal Albert Hall,
So little green-men went to peer,
And saw a crazy ball.

There rows of earthlings sat en masse,
Quite hypnotised and steeled;
By men who blew down tubes of brass
Or scraped till horse-hair squealed.

That morning, Megan and I had held what the Army refers to as an 'O group', a sort of *impromptu* briefing session.

I had bought two basic pay-as-you-go phones in Stratford, again using cash and my Miss Owens driving licence.

I read a psalm, said my prayers and fell asleep.

At eight o'clock, after a bath, I coloured my hair with a medium brown non-permanent hair dye, then fixed it in a bun with a coarse-toothed plastic gripper.

I rubbed some magenta blusher onto my cheeks to hide the pitting, dressed myself in a black A-line linen skirt and a sea-green thigh-length jacket with an internal waist cord, drank tea and packed up my stuff.

With my Barr and Stroud binoculars, I saw in the enemy redoubt, the black and red Roadster, 103 JQL.

With my new pay-as-you-go phone, I rang Megan.

'Dad's at home, so I'll wander up to *The Castle Café*.'

A pair of one-dioptre reading glasses I had bought, added to my disguise.

I locked my rucksack in my car, which was parked under the arches of the nearby railway viaduct.

In the suite occupied by Squibb's Academic Publishing, the reception girl put down her comb.

'Good morning. Could I see a Mr Jason Lacey please?'

'Is he expecting you?'

'No, but it is about an article he reviewed recently.'

'Your name?'

'Ceinlys Dovey.'

She made an internal call. 'He can see you in ten minutes.'

I sat down to wait and sent a message. 'Stand by.' It was acknowledged.

A door opened and Lacey – gold ring in his flabby

lower lip – introduced himself. 'Miss Dovey? I don't recall the name?'

'No. I'm the research assistant for the author in question.'

He led the way through to an open area before steering me into his office. I pressed the 'send' button: 'Five minutes.'

In his late thirties, he had a pigtail, wore sports trousers with an elasticated waist and an Amy Winehouse T-shirt.

'So, what's this about?'

'An article by a Dr Sleight, submitted to your quarterly magazine *The Sounds of Babel*, about the dating of early place names in Norway.'

Lacey opened his palms. 'We receive hundreds of submissions ... '

'This article was *not* reviewed by the editor, Professor Summers, as you stated. Why?'

He gave no reply but leered at my lower body.

I eyed him sternly. 'Well?'

'Well if that's so, I'm sorry. There must have been some mix up.'

'And it has been offered for sale to a professor in Göttingen,' I lied.

'Miss Dovey, there are publishers who handle translations or in syndicating to foreign outlets, but ... '

'Dr Sleight says that yours is the only publishing house to have seen it.'

As Lacey puffed out his cheeks his mobile phone rang. It was his wife haranguing him. The tiler had dropped his hammer into the bath and cracked it.

'Look, I'm with a client ... '

She just shouted over him.

He stood up and walked to the door.

His well-worn A4 address book lay on the desk, fattened with notes and sheets of paper interleaved between its pages. Its disappearance though would be too obvious.

The bottom drawer of the ivy-green sheet-metal filing-cabinet had a pink ticket in its brass label-holder which read 'Foreign'.

'Come on Megan,' I muttered. I was running out of flannel.

Lacey cut his wife off and flopped back into his padded swivel-chair.

'All we needed was a new curtain rail for the shower, but four thousand pounds later ... '

A smart looking girl knocked on the frosted glass panel of his door and popped her head in. 'Jason, a Miss Quigley's on the phone ... about a libel case that's pending?'

He looked puzzled, but said, 'Put it through Lisa ... oh and show Miss Dovey out.'

'What about this pirated article?' I demanded. 'And your dishonest reply to Dr Sleight?'

I had hoped – foolishly I suppose – that he would go to the phone with the incoming call and leave me alone for a time. Instead he gave me a savage smile and hissed, 'Message me with the details ... if you want.'

Megan had rung the Editor-in-Chief's number, not the general reception, then pretended to be the secretary to this lawyer. We had rehearsed the script. When Jason took the phone Megan was to apologise and say that Miss Quigley was on another call and could he hold?

Lisa ushered me out into the open area before indicating the way out.

The reception girl was absent, but the 'Post out' tray was empty and a quick glance round for a key, a pass card or anything which might be useful, drew a blank.

I had a large strong carrier-bag folded up in my shoulder-bag, which I had hoped to fill with goodies, then scurry down the stairs, cross the canal to my car under the low Victorian railway viaduct and execute a K.G.B. style getaway. My visit though, however scrupulously – or unscrupulously – planned, had flopped.

I rang Megan from a motorway hotel.

'I kept him hanging on for *fourteen* minutes.'

'Oh well done ... but it floundered.'

'Oh?' She sounded surprised. 'Still never mind, it was rather living in the fast lane.'

'Well that implies something dodgy, doesn't it?'

'And this wasn't?'

'Well ... it might have looked that way, but the underlying motive was good. Anyway, smash up that phone.'

'Look dear, you're talking to a Bond girl here.'

'Are they particularly bright? Still, they are beautiful.'

With a skirling laugh she cut the call.

*   *   *   *

Washing my hair five or six times removed most of the non-permanent dye. I tied it into its usual two tufts, then drank tea, ate a crusty cheese and tomato baguette and felt more myself.

Remaining undetected is partly a matter of luck.

When Hafid had started convulsing, had I not simply scarpered, but searched him, a lost single blonde hair could at some later date spell my end.

On leaving the DoubleTree Hotel, when the receptionist had had to repeat something, I had replied with some remark about wax in my ears. She then asked what were 'my yurrs'? This was just 'my ears' said with a Welsh accent, but it is a clue which could stick in her mind.

Anyway, as with those metal ingots, I hate giving up.

At ten to six in the evening, a grey mini-bus drew up in the forecourt at Squibb's; 'Summit Cleaning Services'. Six or seven of their employees went into Narrow Boat House with buckets, mops and vacuum-cleaners.

Doing something so obvious that no one would ever think you would be stupid enough to try it, can work.

The mini-bus was left with its back doors open so I helped myself to a grey tabard with their orange logo on it, picked up some thick plastic rubbish bags and followed a few minutes behind the others.

They seemed to be cleaning a number of the office suites. In Squibb's one girl was cleaning the toilets, whilst one of Squibb's own employees sat in the big main office with his feet on a desk, chatting on the phone to his pal.

His back was to me as I slipped into Lacey's office.

I put the A4 address book into a rubbish sack then eyed the filing-cabinet.

I could vaguely hear Ted, the fellow on the phone, chortling. 'Jack thinks he's a bit ahead, but he's actually a lap behind.'

With filing-cabinets, rotating the key usually allows a vertical rod with lugs on it to slide up and engage with notches on the drawers' sides. These locking-bars though are spring-loaded so that a drawer which is still open after locking, can be closed. It will depress the bar briefly as the gradient before its own notch rides over its corresponding lug, pushing it down. Now by walking the cabinet forwards and tilting it backwards you can hopefully pull this bar down ... however, amazingly, it was not locked.

The eighteen folders, in the 'foreign' drawer joined the address book and I tip-toed out.

Ted's scheme to lure some 'sugar-plum fairy', involved he said, not 'a plum' but 'aplomb'.

Back in the motorway hotel, I lay on the bed and stared at the ceiling; too numb to think.

Next day in Harlech, Dad asked what had happened to my hair?

'A new shampoo ... I fell for some advertising gimmick.'

'What's it called, *Cactus-Head*?'

Later Mum served up bowls of bacon and lentil soup, whilst Megan selected a film to watch.

Exit the Vikings is a short comedy. As the Norsemen land on a beach in Northumbria, the Anglo-Saxon thanes reach for their swords and shields, whilst their womenfolk start dabbing on make-up; a bit like modern Britain, where some wish to hold back the invading hordes whilst others welcome them.

Megan was slurping her soup.

'It's lucky you don't go to Roedean.'

'It's usually crunchy cereals which irritate you ... amongst other things.'

'This has even more decibels.'

As she finished it off more quietly, I softened and put my arm round her shoulders. 'Sorry.'

'Why are you putting your arm round me?'

'Because I love you.'

She just grinned. 'Still no boyfriend then?'

The film was just ending.

'No. I do have one.'

'A name?'

'It's a secret, but he calls me "Sweetie pie".'

'Are you his only Sweetie pie? They usually come in boxes of six.'

'Well ... one and a half in this case, but I'm the "one". The half is something unusual.'

'And does "Sweetie pie" have custard poured on top of her from time to time?'

'That's rhubarb or gooseberries ... to neutralise the acid.'

'And you have no acid?'

I laughed briefly. 'It's lucky I'm not easily offended.'

'Bring this guy along. He can have a game of snooker with Dad down at the pub.' Dad is a good snooker player. 'If we tell Dad he's playing him for his daughter's hand, he'll definitely let him win.'

I started pummelling her. She was such a tonic. These fictitious spies never have happy families to sustain them.

After Mum and Dad had gone to bed, I opened my bag and gave Megan three hundred pounds towards her holiday in Switzerland in a week's time. 'Thanks for trying.'

'You do know you're crazy?'

I looked at her. 'I succeeded ... at the second attempt.'

'Oh?'

Megan often did a few chores for Eirwen, our elderly and infirm neighbour.

I fetched a blue plastic storage box from my car.

'When she's nodded off in her chair, could you put this

in her attic? You could stand on a kitchen chair, push back the trap-door and shove it over the coaming?'

She nodded seriously. 'Yes. No one will think to look there. That play, *The Eumenides*? Any chance you'll land a part?'

I sighed. 'I feel cut out for Clytemnestra's Ghost, but ... '

'Was she a queen of Mycenae?'

'Yes.'

'Quite a promotion then? The last time I saw you on stage, you were a scullery maid.'

I blew some bubbles.

* * * *

In Oxford, Matthew came with the inevitable, 'What have you done to your hair?'

I told him about the debacle in Leeds and he looked aghast. 'Sophie, I did not mean you to steal anything.'

'Well what else could we do? They're not going to admit to any funny business?'

I showed him one of the two folders I had kept back.

'I found nothing about your article nor about Judith's, but look at this.'

An article by a Dr Taylor, Reader in Ancient History at Balliol, dealt with Nabataean trade routes in the time of the Herods. It had been retitled, its material somewhat reshuffled and translated, before being sold to a professor in Padua.

'By the way, "Nestor" is one Elaine-Marie Gooch.'

'Ah, "Nestor from Sandy Pylos"?'

He – I think – was an elderly king who sailed with Agamemnon to Troy.

Whilst Matthew read, I made tea and found some French fancies and iced Bakewell tarts in a tin. They looked overly sweet – as their names suggested – but then I spotted a desiccated almond cake.

'That thing's vile,' said Matthew. 'Its centre's bitter.'

I took a nibble. 'Golly! You make it sound better than it is.'

'Margaret Taylor's pretty feisty and her hubby's a lawyer. They'll create havoc with this.'

'Well *good*, that's what we want isn't it? We must copy it, so that she's not "in possession of stolen property".'

'Gooch is on the ethics committee. She looks quite genteel ... like a nineteenth-century porcelain doll ... but she's as hard as nails.'

I imagined a perfect pale face, precisely curved eyebrows, pure yet austere.

I cut some cheese. 'Margaret must say it came anonymously in the post. Ask her to post a large envelope to herself with a stencilled name and address on it ... and say it came in that?'

Matthew's humour had shifted from one of consternation to one of quiet triumph. 'I think we're in business here.'

'There's a lot to sift through, but O'Rourke's name is there too ... probably blocking things from undesirables, rather than selling stuff on.'

Matthew stared at me. 'You're turning out to be quite a bulwark, Sophie.'

I looked down into my cup.

'I had dinner with Roderick last week and said how adept you were at pulling rabbits out of hats ... blue ones, pink ones.'

'Did he say anything?'

'He just smiled.'

I could picture this. 'He likes railways too.'

'I know. In particular, the Furness Railway. The wagon in that painting is grey, but we still don't know the livery of the engines.'

'No.'

'That's the only real gold nugget which we're missing.'

I left him to scan Margaret's rewritten article and the correspondence surrounding it. He then intended to go and see her.

Back in the Annex, Imogen phoned.

'Sophie, would you like to come to France for a few days?'

'Yes ... I'd love to.'

'My father's not well.'

'In what way?'

'Depression.'

'I'm sorry, but ... do you have enough money?'

'A buyer for The National Gallery of Art in Washington called, a Mr Nathan D. Gow – who was one of the judges in Strasbourg – and bought one of my pictures.'

'Not the bread-saw one?'

She tittered. 'I would *never* part with that ... no, *The Watch-tower near Edom*, for five thousand dollars. I had to type out a long description and sign a number of documents.'

'That's a real scoop.'

'It might go into an exhibition in the autumn, he said ... or if not I suppose it'll just disappear into a vault.' She paused. 'If I fix the Eurostar tickets, will you book a hire car in Poitiers?'

'Yes. I'll get onto it.'

I took an afternoon nap and dreamt about sheep. A farmer near Bala drove a bleating flock of Llanwenogs through a gate.

'Does the lambing season depend on when you put the rams in with the ewes?' I asked.

He laughed. 'No. They don't come on heat until the weather warms up ... so spring-time.'

Eirig knocked. Someone had let him in.

As I stood up and rubbed my eyes, he handed me a parcel which the postman had brought and a bunch of wild roses. 'They grow beside the railway.'

'Thank you.'

'I just felt I needed to see you.'

'You're looking a touch under-cuddled.'

I hugged him and we toppled onto the bed where we kissed and caressed for a time. As he fingered my hair, he asked predictably, 'What's happened?'

I told him of the failed half of the Leeds story. 'It was just a shot in the dark.'

'Worse things happen at sea.'

'I'm often too impetuous.'

'Nelson said, "Delay favours the defender."'

In the kitchen, I washed up an empty jam jar to hold the roses.

'I'll cook us a student meal. Do you know what that is?'

'Mouldy bread and someone else's cheese?'

'No. It means you scrape all your left-overs into a saucepan, add a few dubious herbs, heat it up and give it a foreign name.'

I unwrapped the parcel. It was a book I had ordered on sheep farming.

'Eirig, do you know anything about sheep farming?'

'No.'

'Well neither did Beatrix Potter, but that didn't stop her from doing it.'

After our stew of oddments, I read the book's first paragraph aloud. 'The mild yet moist maritime climate of the British Isles – combined with its good soil – gives much excellent pasture. It depends though on the grazing of sheep or the rearing of cattle to keep it free of bracken, brambles or thorns.'

Eirig's visit and the Leeds episode had buoyed me up.

Satisfaction often comes from finally fighting the battles which we have tried to dodge.

We held each other very tightly that night, though at four thirty Eirig – being on a six o'clock shift – had to rise, shine and leave.

Around mid-morning the door-bell rang. I tripped downstairs to find a nervous looking youth stood on the step.

'I'm Duncan. Is Emma in?'

I knocked on her panelled blue door and we waited, though I knew her to be in Apulia.

'No. Would you like to wait ... and have a cup of tea?'

We joined Alison in the kitchen, where she was eating a cheese bun with some fat spring onions. 'Hi ham heating honions,' she breathed heavily at us, before giving Duncan a twisted smile. 'You're not *still* besotted with her?'

He gave a forlorn nod.

She turned to me. 'Moon-struck is an understatement. He keeps asking her out, but either she comes up with some cock-and-bull excuse or – more harshly – just tells him to buzz off.'

I took this in. 'You must not *appear* desperate,' I urged. 'That's always a mistake.'

As I put the tea-mugs on the table, Alison expanded. 'My gut instinct though is that Emma does feel something for you deep down, but since you don't fit with her ambitions, she wants to scare you off?'

I blinked. 'A trifle convoluted? So their failure to coalesce – as you think *should* happen – will seem to be Duncan's fault?'

'That is *exactly* right,' Duncan's voice shuddered with emphasis.

Alison mused, 'She's keen to work abroad ... to see the world ... '

We all fell silent ... and Duncan left.

He let himself out and we heard the main door close.

Alison said, 'His surname's "Seymour". Perhaps our advice will help him to "see more" than would an optician?'

Perhaps there was a joke in there somewhere.

I asked seriously, 'Is it folly, that he's so persistent?'

'I don't know.'

'It's an unusual but striking form of romanticism ... or self-knowledge.'

'Emma though, is rumoured ... '

I held up a hand. 'Let's leave it there. One piece of gossip is enough?'

Alison left for a violin lesson and soon afterwards the door-bell rang again.

Stroppy Poppy stood on the door-step. She managed a plasticky but civil smile. 'Someone important would like to meet with you.'

'Oh.'

'Professor O'Rourke.'

'What about?'

'He didn't specify the topic.'

'Well ... tell him that if he could kindly supply an agenda, I will be happy to oblige.'

She turned and left.

Twenty minutes later, the bell rang again. Was there a queue out there?

When I opened the door, I found no one. I walked out into the lane but saw nobody.

As I packed my bag for France, I had a feeling that things were going on under the surface of a quite sinister nature ... and I did not think it was all to do with Squibb's.

CHAPTER EIGHT

In Paris we caught a train from the Gare Montparnasse to Poitiers, where at the car rental desk I presented the form for the car I had booked, a modest Renault Clio.

'Would you like to upgrade to a bigger car?'

'No thanks.'

'Would you like a bigger car anyway?'

'No thanks.'

'Well, we only have a bigger car.'

I viewed the extremely long-nosed Citroën. 'Luckily I'm long-sighted.'

'*Pardon?*'

'Which end can we saw off?'

We drove out southwards along the N11. These old *Routes Nationales* had once had evenly-spaced plane trees along one verge, such that shadows flicked across you, but these were now gone.

The countryside here was mildly undulating and with quite a lot of woodland.

Imogen confided in me. 'Daddy – like Uncle Matthew – inherited a large sum in 2010 when my grandfather died. He sent me to private school whilst he came to France and bought – but probably paid too much for – this lovely old country house. He was then led down the garden path by a French *aventurière* and I think lost further sums gambling at the casino in Monte Carlo. He now struggles. There's a *gîte* which he rents out and he helps a local builder tile roofs.'

Just before the village of Coulombiers, a baker's van stopped abruptly at a house and I bumped it, though only lightly. Its driver climbed out, surveyed the dent and – as I began to apologise – gave the stock Gallic shrug and waved us on.

'Oh well,' said Imogen, 'at least you've shortened it a bit.'

I mentioned the Squibb escapade. 'The timing of this holiday could be spot-on.'

She smiled. 'Shrewd diplomats are never around when the balloon goes up. Perhaps Matthew had an inkling of the same. He's gone to Barnard Castle. He thought to go to Stockholm, but in the area where his friend lives there are huge race riots and arson attacks going on.'

'Goodness.'

'They've called out the army ... and this, not long ago, was almost a crime-free country.'

We turned left and crossed the railway.

Imogen's father's house, *Le Manoir des Cerisiers*, had been solidly built with grey-brown roughly-hewn stone ashlars, but gutted in 1944 by the Gestapo, when its owner was suspected of hiding members of *la Résistance*. It had been well-renovated though and had wavy orange roof-tiles and new oak window-frames with grey and white diagonally striped shutters which gave it a slightly heraldic or historic aura. It was not particularly large, so perhaps a grange rather than a manor.

In a meadow to one side stood the neat little *gîte* and a few sheep and on the other side an untended overgrown orchard, whilst pretty lupins bordered the path up to the front door.

Jolyon – Imogen's father – was quite evidently dejected. She hugged him and tried to kindle some reciprocal warmth with a degree of success.

He apologised to me and said that he still missed his wife, despite the twelve-year gap.

'Pappa, there's no need to say that. Even when we're at our best, it's never good enough for the wrong person, but the right person will still always understand you.'

He managed a smile. 'And you're the right person?'

She looked at him.

'Your mother wasn't.'

'No, I know.'

Younger than Matthew, he lacked his bother's gravity or solid self-belief and – perhaps like the Prodigal Son – still yearned for the parties and the bonhomie of times past.

Matthew still owned six houses in Carlisle and quite a number of farms.

Jolyon had prepared a 'fricassee Languedoc', basically a beef stew with lashings of rosemary and thyme and some wine in it.

Under the gnarled beams of the low long kitchen, Imogen told how Mr Gow's purchase had enabled her to come and visit him.

'It was a piece of course-work, but because its dimensions were fractionally over those cited in the syllabus's regulations, it was marked down heavily.'

'By whom?'

'This nabob, Raju Datir, Lecturer in Early Indic Art. He's so poor, goodness knows how he landed the job. If he draws a banana you can't tell what it is.'

'Perhaps there's a requirement for "diversity"?'

'I daresay that's it.'

We all took a second ladle of stew. Apparently in France it is bad manners to refuse a second serving. A third helping is optional whilst a fourth is considered greedy.

'He's the treasurer too for a charity collecting money to build a Hindu temple and is alleged to have embezzled its funds.'

We all laughed.

'Aren't these guys just fantastic?' I remarked.

On the morning of our second day, since Imogen was trying to encourage her father to overcome his loneliness, I offered to go with Cédric Joubert the builder and so spent the day in the summer sunshine in the French countryside.

When my basic French was insufficient to grasp what was required, a brief demonstration usually sufficed.

I cleaned the mortar off lots of curved old orange-coloured roof tiles. Being lime mortar it fell away easily enough with a hammer and a cold chisel.

After lunch – which was sausage, Brie and a half of a baguette with some very rough *vin de table* wine – I mixed mortar; four of sand to one of cement, with plasticiser and water as necessary.

Both Jolyon and Eirig lived alone, yet one was lonely and the other not. We are all wired differently.

When on the roof of this barn, I gazed out over meadows and hedgerows and saw sheep, barley and distant low hills.

Cédric I sensed, from a glance he threw me, did not think well of his client, a showy old *pied-noir* who wore a ring on his finger with a diamond the size of an Oxo cube and whose sports car had leopard-skin seat-covers. He had too gold tooth fillings and used the title 'Comte', which though not against French law – since all noble titles had been abolished during the revolution – was none the less very affected.

Over dinner, Imogen said after reading a psalm, 'The oldest Semitic word for "god" is the letter "l" preceded by a vowel with a smooth breathing. It is "il" in Babylon, "el" in Israel and "ilah" in Arabia. "Allah" is "ilah" preceded by the definite article "al" and compressed. This was their word for the Jewish and Christian God before Islam came on the scene.'

Next day Imogen and I took the train to Paris. She had been asked by a wealthy German to paint an enlarged copy of the head of 'Astronomy', a detail from a group of Muses painted by Botticelli. It hangs in the Louvre, where Imogen studied the original and made notes.

'She's a little *too* sweet,' I said, eyeing her *faux-naïf* expression with its affectedly lowered eyelids, upturned nose, wimple and caduceus.

On the morrow, in the summer-house, Imogen started sketching *Astronomy*, whilst I – wearing a pair of thick old gauntlets – trimmed a wild-looking bramble hedge on one side of the orchard and fed all the twigs into an industrial grade electric shredder.

I remembered the phrase, *Les mûres devant le mur sont mûres*; 'The blackberries in front of the wall are ripe.'

Imogen and I drove to Limoges, but lost our way. We saw a sign which read, *Travaux*. We studied a map, looking for this village until we realised that *Travaux* meant 'Road works'. At a cross-roads in a small town our indecision caused a traffic jam and a gendarme called across, '*Avancez, s'il vous plaît.*' When we explained where we trying to go, he smiled, indicated the turn required and said, '*Prenez la rue de Saint-Junien.*'

We were – as you might say – 'brushing up' our French.

Imogen was nervous about my driving and remarked after every trip, how to her astonishment it had been ding-free or dent-free. I replied that the car had a genie which loved it.

In Poitiers, the Baptistery of Saint John dated back to Merovingian times and the baptismal font sunk into its floor, from a still earlier fourth-century Roman villa. It was a proto-Romanesque structure, in its mix of stone and thin bricks or tiles, quite unlike our Saxon churches. A deep tranquillity permeated its interior. We studied its murals, Biblical scenes whose colours were plain, dusky and chalky.

In *L'Orangerie* we chose the *table d'hôte* menu. Its first course was a Viennese schnitzel, potatoes, cabbage and white sauce. Whilst waiting, I wrote my second postcard to Eirig. I knew now that we were happy together and with my whole mind and body, felt a sort of certainty about the future.

I said to Imogen what a lovely change it had been to skidding round England and I thanked her for asking me.

She smiled. *'Nous sommes les bonnes amies.'*

*   *   *   *

Megan was cutting a wisdom tooth.

At two in the morning she stood up to take some soluble aspirin.

Before she had switched the kitchen light on, the lights of a vehicle swept by and a Transit van drew up at the end of our little dead-end road.

Outside it was dark, moonless and misty. Occasional gusts shook the windows.

Mum had gone to stay with Grandma, so the Land Rover was absent.

A young woman pressed the door-bell, but Megan held down the little hammer which would usually vibrate against the round grey bell. Skeleton keys turned the lock of the kitchen door, but it had two substantial bolts.

Megan shook Dad and told him to get up.

Then came the faint scraping of a thin flexible metal strip being inserted between the front door and its frame. It eased the catch back, but the trespasser – a flimsy youth – met unexpectedly with Dad, who grabbed him by the throat, rotated him, then rammed his face against the side of the house. Megan turned on some lights. The trespasser's nose poured blood and as he fell backwards, his maroon turban rolled across the ground.

His female accomplice just managed to dial 999 before Dad gripped her by the scruff or her neck, applied what is known as a 'Spanish windlass' to her collar and held her up like a hang-dog corpse dangling from a gallows.

Had a vulture circled overhead I wondered, in anticipation of some nice juicy carrion?

The van drove away, although Megan caught its number plate.

The woman squirmed and squealed and told Dad he was 'crossing a red line'.

Megan took photos of the captives, extracted their wallets and took pictures also of their driving licences.

Two police constables arrived in a patrol car with its blue light flashing, grasped the general thread of events, then pointed out that as the would-be burglars had not *actually* crossed the threshold, the only person they could charge would be Dad, for 'assault'.

Megan had to physically restrain him from seizing the police officer, but he informed him none the less via a few pithy epithets, that he should go and jump in the sea.

When the ambulance drew up, Mostafa Khan gave its crew a false name.

Dad muttered, 'This lot aren't called shites for nothing.'

'That comment Sir, could be seen as racist.'

The woman – having now recovered her self-confidence – looked down her nose at Dad, possibly to deliberately egg him on.

He growled, 'If I had a detonator, I'd shove it up ... '

Megan clapped a hand over his mouth. 'Shut up!'

Since Dad stood like an ox in the furrow, the police left without further ado, taking the woman with them.

As he and Megan drank tea, he asked, 'What were they up to? We've no gold ingots here?'

Megan shrugged.

'What third-rate policemen too. They should express themselves clearly, but *not* smoothly.'

Megan added, 'Not a defect which you suffer from.'

She studied the card photos. 'Goodness, Elaine-Marie Gooch is a Reverend Canon.'

'Would Sophie know anything about this?'

'Hmm ... I shouldn't think so.'

'Where is she?'

'In France,' Megan uttered tartly.

'And tomorrow you're off to Switzerland?'

'So you'll be holding the fort?'

He sensed she was keeping something back. 'Out with it?'

'Well, just don't kill too many besiegers.'

*   *   *   *

I accompanied Matthew to his hearing.

'Ninth floor,' said the porter.

There is a Noël Coward saying, 'The higher the building, the lower the morals.'

The chair, Dame Melissa Opoku O.B.E., Professor of Sub-Saharan Philosophy, introduced her 'team'.

'Dr Raju Datir for the academic staff, Dr Musa Eze our sociologist and Poppy Toogood our student representative.'

We nodded woodenly.

The hearing lacked any format or numbered sequence. With some legal knowledge, I could probably have objected to this gimcrack set-up.

The plaintiff had been excused too, since she was 'too emotionally distressed'.

'We wished to show empathy,' Opoku chided us as we stared blankly. Were we meant to applaud this display of showy 'humanity'?

'Sympathy' is 'suffering with', but 'suffering in' seems to make no sense, etymologically at least.

Our silence I think irritated these solipsistic owls. Opoku handed the baton to Dr Eze.

Allegedly, in his study, Matthew had slid his hand along this girl's thigh and up under her skirt.

'Her name?' I asked.

'It's confidential ... for her safety.'

'Dr Sleight would surely know it?'

'Not necessarily.'

'It will be Naomi Southern,' Matthew stated. 'I have a C.C.T.V. photograph here of her leaving Exeter College

143

four minutes after this supposed incident.' He laid a grainy black and white photo on the table, its date and time printed on it.

'Do you have permission to access such?' Datir quizzed with a twinge of petulance.

Matthew, being on friendly terms with the porters, had asked them to search the recordings for him.

'Which porter gave you this?' snapped Opoku querulously.

'Er ... I forget, but please examine it.'

'Your point?'

'She's wearing jeans ... not a skirt,' I said.

After a dead silence, Opoku, suddenly unsure of her ground but with bulging blood-shot eyes, picked up a spongy rubber ball, a tension-reliever in the form of the head of a white male and squeezed it.

In Waterstone's coffee-shop, I remarked, 'Poor stage-management.'

'You never entirely win. This will be kept on record to provide "context" at any future hearing ... a lead-in to the anxious frowns of "concern".'

We cut in half a smoked salmon and scrambled-egg panino and shared a half-bottle of white wine.

'Naomi was hardly a cracker. I thought they might charge you with bad taste?'

He smiled. 'I wonder how they paid her?'

'If life was only about toy trains?'

'Perhaps in heaven it will be?'

I thought of God ... my wonderful and good God. 'I sometimes dream about having a small farm ... with sheep.'

'Closer to nature?'

'It sounds trite ... but yes.'

Students made up most of the café's clientele, for summer holidays aside, there are resits, research projects or just a wish not to be at home.

Matthew, prodded his salmon. 'In the Scandinavian tongues, "lax" or a variant of it, is the word for "salmon" and its wide geographical spread has seen it cited in theories about early migrations.'

'You can learn too from Viking raids? From pillage or rape ... coin hoards, genetic traits?'

'And the lesson of the Danegeld ... if anyone today cares to reflect.'

I put a finger to my lips.

'The word *vik* means "inlet". So the Vikings are possibly "the inlet people".'

I mentioned Imogen's 'Ruth' painting. 'I've watched it progress. A light touch ... and you can sense the breeze wafting through the corn.'

'From the age of ten, she wanted to paint ... and from the age of fifteen, to learn Biblical Hebrew.'

'It's unusual to be so single-minded so early in life?'

*   *   *   *

That afternoon, Judith came to the Annex.

'My sister-in-law's had a weird experience.'

'Go on.'

'Her land-line phone rang and when she answered, it was an answering machine which relayed a recorded message. It stated, "Jake's given the green light. Friday. Operation *Bon-bon* is on."'

'Sorry, I'm not with this.'

'It cut off abruptly and Stephanie thinks it was some sort of unintended play-back ... that it was sent to her in error.'

I thought for a time. 'Do you think it was deliberate ... a goad to make her panic?'

'I asked the same, but she said it had not felt engineered or spurious.'

'So what is "Operation *Bon-bon*"?'

'We don't know.'

'Let's make tea.'

'She tried to book a flight to Italy, but her passport's been invalidated.'

'I've a baguette in the fridge. Shall we share it?'

'No ham or bacon?'

'Cheese and tomato.'

When we were settled, she said, 'I called on her in her little skewed Hansel-and-Gretel house. I disguised myself with an orange cycle helmet and a pizza box ... as if I were a delivery girl.'

This sounded a touch amateur.

'Lights were on and as I walked up the short garden path, she opened the door, accepted the pizza and beckoned me inside.

I asked why she did not just drive off at three in the morning and go to Scotland, but she said they would be able to track her.'

'That's probably true.'

'Later I hid in Saint Wulfstan's churchyard, in long grass between a holly bush and a tilted grave-stone and watched the path to her cottage for a long time.'

I stared at her. 'Judith, we have no chance at this sort of game. These M.I.6 guys are very good at stealth and surveillance ... not S.A.S. standard, but still very good. They would pick us up long before we spotted them.'

She hung her head slightly in acknowledgement of this.

We drank tea, divided the baguette and were still for a time.

'But we do know the day ... *this* Friday ... could you go and watch ... and possibly stop whatever it is?'

I looked at her.

'You say you've no experience – but what about faith ... prayer? We believe in a true and just God. We ought not to despair, to become dispirited?'

I inhaled then breathed out slowly.

'Gerard's found a lovely property at Atlit. He rang and asked me to pop out so I did. It's a little way south of Haifa, newish ... but with a dash of character and colour added it could be really swish. It's almost on the beach and with three rooms which we could let. So we made on offer and it's been accepted.'

'Good. Something to be cheerful about. I'll come and visit you one day.'

'Yes, I do hope so.'

I saw her out.

*　　*　　*　　*

I mowed the small lawn in our back garden, put out our only deck-chair and – with a milk-shake beside me – reread *The Eumenides*.

It starts in Delphi. The Furies, those primeval hag-like

spectres, are pursuing Orestes. Apollo though, fed up with their shrieks and howls and wanting an afternoon nap, has put them into a stupor.

The monologue by Clytemnestra's Ghost could, I thought, be executed with a touch of comedy, an air of, 'Hey you dozy lumps, you're *supposed* to be scaring my son, who's *murdered* me ... Matricide? Remember?'

Under the garden shed and wrapped in black plastic, lay the last of the three precious metal bars I had taken from the cast-iron pipe in Northumberland. Using a hoe, I had pushed it a long way in and surrounded it with dead leaves and other dirt, which had gathered there. The shed's bearers rested on thin bricks so there had been just enough space to manoeuvre it in.

Megan, bored with D. H. Lawrence – after drinking most of my milk-shake – wanted a game of chess.

'The guy's in love with his mother ... how weird is that?'

When a rook and a bishop down, I capitulated.

'So? How does the play end?' she asked.

'In the last scene, Athena persuades the Furies to no longer be "bloodthirsty avengers", but to relent and each one instead to become a *eu-menos*, a kindly spirit.'

I wondered how much effort Stephanie's pursuers were putting into shadowing me? If you are not actually up to anything though, then it is immaterial.

Megan and I knocked on our neighbour's door. It was unlocked – as it always is – so we tip-toed in. Eirwen was asleep in her chair, so in her kitchen – the building is a bungalow – I took the box of files from Squibb's from her attic and put it in my car, whilst Megan touched Eirwen's arm to wake her and then made cups of tea and we sat down to listen to stories of Sunday-school trips to Chester Zoo and Girl Guide hikes in the Brecon Beacons.

I drove to Uncle Hywel's, where in his comfy garden shed, I settled down to study the contents of my box more thoroughly.

Over tea he asked, 'What about that dead fellow in Harlech yesterday?'

'Sorry, what dead fellow?'

In a field on the north-eastern edge of the town, a man dressed in good quality countryman-style clothes had been charged by a herd of cattle. He had shot one but then apparently been overwhelmed and was later discovered with his neck broken and with both his head and his telescope trampled into the mud. His name was given as Roger Stubbs from Lewes in Sussex.

'The farmer, Dennis Williams, had once bred a more docile breed, but it frequently miscalved ... so he changed to this other one – whose name begins with an "r" – which rarely miscalves but is known to be quite aggressive.'

I stuck labels and coloured tabs onto the jigsaw of exchanges and agreements from Squibb's. The codenames – used in correspondence – Clio, Argon and Nestor, I had already solved by cross-referencing the addresses on the letters to the address book. O'Rourke, Lacey and Gooch were solidly implicated.

And in amongst it all, was a remarkable stepping-stone, a jump perhaps to something I so quixotically longed for.

Next day I button-holed Dad. 'Dad, will you help me?'

He sensed my earnest.

'I think my car might have a tracker on it. Do you know how to find them?'

'We had them in Ireland, but that's some years back.'

I waited.

'They didn't transmit if stationary, so you had to search physically.'

'Go on.'

'Most are magnetic, so you put them on the bodywork behind the bumper say or underneath on the side of the petrol tank.'

He had two little ramps in the shed for when he changed the oil in the Land Rover.

'Can you check the Polo for me?'

'Is this to do with that break-in?'

'No ... but you *mustn't* say anything.'

I offered to trim the hedge and did an excellent job.

'I've found two.'

'Two?!'

He gave me a rough but very tight hug and I knew that he knew.

CHAPTER NINE

I set off for Stroud in the Land Rover. In a petrol station I popped the trackers into a folded tarpaulin on the back of a lorry which had an address in Aberdeen on its cab sides.

Outside the flats where Eirig lived, I met the woman with the dog ... or rather it met me. It was smallish and yappy and wanted to gnaw my ankle, though its owner held it back on its leash.

'Are you Eirig's girlfriend?'

'Yes.'

'That doll ... is she a lure?'

'A lure?'

'Yes. To lure small children?'

Quite an opener this, to someone you have never spoken to before. I gave a muffled groan. 'Isn't this a sad world?'

She stepped back. 'I'm a social worker.'

'I might have guessed.'

'And we have to be alert to such things.'

'Oh.'

'Why does he have a her?'

'She does the housework.'

She gave a melodramatic huff through gritted teeth.

'Someone as gentle and harmless as Eirig ... have you no ability to judge character?'

Her dog now wanted to bite the driver of a grocery delivery van.

Inside, Eirig said, 'It's so lovely when you come.'

He began to reheat some charred dried-out lasagne,

but his lighting a candle, his cuddles and a little romantic persiflage did enough to make me happy.

After a time we binned the lasagne, blew out the candle, went for a walk and bought fish and chips.

On our return we again met the woman with the yappy dog.

'This was in my mail-box. It's yours.'

It was a railway magazine called *Steam Days*.

'Lucky it's not *Steamy Days*?' she sniggered.

'Do you think that's funny?'

She shrugged. 'Yes I do, actually.'

Inside, on the sofa, we read from my sheep farming book, the section on hedges; how to extend and nurture them so as to provide shelter for animals and a habitat for birds and butterflies. It mentioned 'laying'. If there is a gap, by cutting the thinner stems part-way through and bending them over and fixing them down, you can over a few years, restore the continuity and thickness of a damaged hedge.

The intercom buzzed.

'Soffie Ooze here no?'

Puzzled, we went down to the lobby to meet two policemen; a coloured sergeant and a white constable.

The sergeant wore a dark blue turban with the constabulary's E II R silver badge on it. He spoke in a deep level monotone; its syllables regular, unstressed and of equal length. I have heard languages like this before, very rhythmical, like a water pump throbbing quietly away.

'Soffie we told to see you if is here hair blonde and sometime violet.'

'Violet?'

'Violent,' the constable clarified.

'If agitated told to arrest you damaging the state isn't it?'

I asked to see their warrants – which appeared to be genuine – and mentally noted their collar numbers. 'Well, I'm here ... though without the magenta hair. What next?'

'Men in suits high up to know if you here good suits ask rank men.'

'Savile Row? But who *were* they?'

'From capital want us you to check.'

'London? With what sort of authority?'

The explanation given was so broken as to be unintelligible, though one phrase sounded like, 'Emma eyes sex.'

The constable exhaled softly and tapped his colleague's boot with his own. Clearly this bone-headed sergeant was giving away stuff he was not meant to.

'I'm sorry, but I can't understand you at all. Isn't competence in English a part of the police recruitment process any more?'

'Why you cross haff round neck?' This came in a more aggressive tone.

'Because I'm Christian,' I said softly, but eyed him sternly.

'That is offence if it to insult somebody ... '

A message came over his radio. A lady walking her dogs had seen a girl being forced to the ground by three young coloured men behind The Canal Trust's visitor centre.

The officers looked at one another.

'Do we go?' asked the constable.

'What if Moslems in group two orders?'

'I think for rape we're supposed to attend, Sergeant.'

They hesitated, then left without a farewell. They climbed into their van, but only after two minutes did they drive off. Would they put their blue light and siren on to warn the possible culprits of their approach? Ah yes, they thought of that.

I once heard of an officer who had arrived at such a scene by rolling down a hill after turning his car's engine and lights off; old-style policing, using 'The Ways and Means Act'.

I rang the police station who confirmed, from the names and collar numbers, that the officers were bona fide. I asked the reason for their visit. The police girl went away and then returned. 'We think it was some sort of Home Office query.'

I thanked her.

Eirig slept face-down, his right arm across my chest.

Moonlight filtered through the unlined curtains. I turned on my side, put my arms around my sleeping beloved and hugged him tightly.

We human beings are a pretty shabby lot, although most of us do a fair job of disguising it. My faith though is such that I know that God is omnipresent and that contentment depends on integrity, which in practice means being clear about what you should be, about the path you should be treading ... and trying hard to stick to it.

I had set the alarm for three.

*   *   *   *

I left Dad's Land Rover hidden in a plantation of young firs at twenty past six; just after sunrise.

I walked to the twisty country lane which ran roughly parallel to Cumberford's main street. If I heard a vehicle, I ducked into the woodland on the upper side of the road and bent down until it had passed.

A bridleway ran downhill from this lane for six hundred yards, until after skirting Stephanie's cottage, it continued for another two hundred into the village.

A cool early mist still hovered over the fields.

If you do not know how to move silently, then the golden rule has to be not to move.

Apart from a few saplings and fences and the ragged road-side hedge, the landscape was quite open.

A fallen tree trunk had lain unmoved for some time, judging by the thick crusts of sedge and moss on it. Last autumn's leaves though were now dry and crisp and potentially noisy. Kneeling behind it too would only give an overview of the first downhill part of the bridleway.

The answer lay with an open-sided hay barn, backed by a single oak. It consisted of a concrete floor, six vertical metal girders and a curved reddy-brown metal roof. It was two-thirds-full of oblong hay bales, so I climbed up onto the upper ones which were about twelve feet above the ground, snuggled myself into a slight depression between two of them and fluffed up some loose stalks to shield my face. Assuming that I was here before 'they' were, this seemed quite good.

In Stephanie's partly shrub-hidden cottage, a light flickered. Perhaps she would be making breakfast?

As time passed and the warmth of the overcast day

grew, I removed my khaki-green canvas jacket and olive-green woollen bobble hat and managed with difficulty to pour myself a cup of tea.

At around nine o'clock a maroon people carrier came along the lane. I watched its roof as it stopped in a passing-place to let a tractor by. It then resumed its journey.

The hedge impeded my view of the lane, but almost immediately a second tractor appeared, stopped and its driver waved someone across the road. Someone had been dropped off by that people carrier.

I felt a slight sweat break out on my forehead.

I rested my chin on my hat, hoped my hair looked like hay and prepared to draw back a little if the enemy came close.

I scanned everywhere with my ex-army binoculars but could spot no movement. Were the new arrivals going over their plan or checking their kit?

A tall youngish white fellow and a girl of similar build – both dressed as hikers – appeared suddenly on the bridleway below me.

A squirrel scurrying across the roof above me scared me, its claws scratching the metal.

I managed to take a photo, though at fifty yards it would give no real detail, even though set to two-times magnification. I had also set it to superimpose the date and time on each shot.

The hikers strolled up to Stephanie's front door and rang the bell.

I took a second shot, but this time at over a hundred yards.

As Stephanie answered and let the callers in, I wondered if she knew what was coming, but had decided to acquiesce and not to fight?

Had I brought her pistol along and tried to intervene, what would have been the outcome? Perhaps I would have shot somebody, then been tried by a judge who swallowed all the government's lies and put me in gaol?

On the positive side though, these interlopers clearly did not know that I was there.

A house sparrow alighted beside me briefly and somewhere a horse neighed.

As the wickedness of it all sank into my mind, my heart-rate rose.

An hour passed before the front door opened and out came the two ramblers. They looked around, checked that the door was firmly locked, then headed in my direction, back toward the twisty lane. I took a photo from almost overhead and another of their backs at twenty-yards, but had not risked a frontal shot for fear of being spotted.

They paused. The girl must have felt too hot. She took off her rucksack, her jacket and her woolly, before putting her jacket back on. On the front of her woolly, I picked out using my binoculars, a large scarab embroidered in orange and blue thread.

Then, to my astonishment, a sturdy fellow with a shoulder-high Alpine walking-stick, which I took to be a theatrical prop, popped up from behind the very tree trunk which I had dismissed; a sentry, an outlying picket.

I took another long-range shot as he jabbed at his telephone. After a few minutes a white BMW picked the threesome up where the bridleway joined the lane. It was sideways on and so I could not read its number, but I took yet another long-range photo.

I had risen at three that morning and exhausted, I

unintentionally fell asleep.

It was midday when I awoke. The church clock was still striking the hour.

I surveyed the whole area carefully for fifteen minutes, then hotched down the hay bales to land amid a sea of tall purple foxgloves.

Eirwen took digoxin, which she said came from the leaves of the purple foxglove. Although a small amount could alleviate heart failure, overdosing is harmful and the therapeutic dose is close to the toxic dose ... I remembered her saying.

Still exercising caution, I made for Dad's Land Rover.

When I found it, I froze. Beside it was a swish modern Land Rover, not I thought a farmer's vehicle.

Then I saw that a man sat in the driver's seat and approaching warily, I realised that he was asleep.

It was Roderick. I rapped on the glass. He stirred, climbed out and took my hand, covering our joined right hands with his left.

'Where were you?'

'On top of those hay bales.'

He nodded. 'Did you take any pictures?'

'Yes, but no close-ups.'

'I took pictures too, but only of their vehicles. Print off your stuff, hide it, then delete the originals from your phone. We won't do anything for a bit.'

'It might be best not to do anything ever ... it will almost certainly just be squashed.'

Roderick nodded slowly. 'Well, let's see.'

We drove off separately.

*   *   *   *

Matthew naturally had written the text for his book, but I was busy with a list of changes when the College porter knocked with the mail.

Matthew – after re-appearing with two coffees – opened the first letter and gave a gasp of surprise. 'That article of mine; it's to be published.'

'Good,' I said with some emphasis.

'Most large farms in Scandinavia broke up into smaller or more isolated homesteads early in the Christian era, probably due to a worsening climate. I narrowed this down to soon after 400 A.D. by dating this second wave of names by time-fixed linguistic shifts; the assimilation of paired consonants or the loss of an initial "w" for example.'

'Good,' I repeated.

'When Margaret Taylor's hubby put the squeezers on this Elaine-Marie Gooch, she initially went nuts ... but then yielded and agreed to parley.'

'So both Margaret's article and yours are to be published?'

'A sop to keep us quiet.'

'Excellent. It's good when push-back succeeds.'

He broke the seal of the special delivery letter, the one which the porter had had to sign for.

'It's from Professor M. O. Opoku O.B.E. ... lots of fiery cant ... but my sex-abuse case has been dropped.'

'More good news.'

Her signature consisted of huge squiggles, like an adder looping its way across a meadow. The tapering off of the first and last strokes showed the pen to have been moving at speed as it hit or came off the page. 'There's a small hole there where the nib's punctured the paper and thrown off a spray of ink droplets.'

I had ordered a copy of a seventy-page document held in The University of Michigan's library. It had arrived in my inbox and I read its title aloud: 'Observations on the Proposed Railway from Newcastle-upon-Tyne to North ... '

Matthew started to choke on his ginger-nut. It seemed to go on for ages.

'Shall I stop and read a psalm? This after all is perhaps not the last thing you wish to hear during your earthly sojourn?'

When he finally recovered his ability to speak, he said with a crooked smile, 'You cheeky thing.'

Over my shoulder, Matthew scrolled down the survey. 'It lists the necessary land purchases ... and gives the engineer's track design specifications ... ' He broke off.

'Oh and this,' I pointed. '*Quod vide*: an attached revision says the engines ordered from Hawthorn's were to be painted dark green and not Prussian blue as first stated.'

'So, our last conundrum's solved?'

Lastly, a birthday card from a cousin in Whitehaven, read simply, 'Love from Clare.'

'Is it your birthday?'

He blushed faintly. 'Fifty-six.'

He had booked a table at a top-notch country hostelry for himself and Imogen that evening, but he rang up and changed it to three.

In the Annex, that afternoon, I had a surprise visitor.

Elaine-Marie Gooch, the college chaplain at Newlove, came to warn me about the fires of hell.

'Sophie, someone dealt you a rogue ace ... but that's now been cashed in.'

I had been having a nap and was a little dazed. 'Oh ... ?'

'All in authority here now hold progressive views.'

'Er ... or have to pretend to?'

'So no room for oddballs ... not active ones anyway?' A disparaging grin formed on her face. 'So be sensible, toe the line. ... *Pioneer?*'

I almost said, 'What?' but realised just in time that she thought this was my undercover codename. I gave a resigned sigh as if owning up, a false admission which might cover for the real *Pioneer?*

I moved on. 'Why is Imogen Sleight a target? She's not fighting you?'

'I think that's an academic issue, not a political one.'

'She's often abused too for wearing a cross round her neck and none of you stands up for her.'

'If she rubs people up the wrong way, then ... '

I exhaled. 'I don't see you being burnt at the stake for your convictions?'

Elaine-Marie lowered her tone to a gravelly one. 'In a multi-cultural world, a degree of sensitivity is required.'

I was wearing the rough hessian dress and rope waist-tie left over from *Y Tywysog*. 'You should try wearing sack-cloth and ashes,' I pointed, 'like the townsfolk of Nineveh?'

At seven, Matthew, Imogen and I arrived at *Le Manoir aux Quat' Saisons*, a fifteenth century manor surrounded by beautifully tended walled gardens, dovecots and statues.

The starter, an exquisite twice-baked haddock sorbet, was followed by a tender fillet steak which melted on your tongue.

I told of my afternoon caller. We all knew that we were being coerced into silence and were probably the butt of olde *worlde* jokes.

Matthew bowed his head.

'Do you remember Katie, the girl with the arms-smuggler boyfriend from Central America? Well, she married him and he's now the deputy defence minster there. It seems she had more intuition or grasp of reality, than I gave her credit for.'

'As long as she's not gunned down next week?' I coughed on the wine.

Matthew studied the label. '*Un fiasco di Calabria*.' He sipped it and grimaced. 'Imogen, why did you choose this? Have you no palate ... apart from your paint palette?'

She managed a weak laugh. 'I liked the picture on its label.'

'That is *not* the way to choose wine.'

She pondered briefly. 'A Buddhist achieves enlightenment through meditation and self-denial, whilst this Katie reaches it with two gin and tonics and some starry-eyed banter?'

'Perhaps we're missing a trick?' I queried.

Matthew reflected. 'It seems incongruous, but often students who are academically gifted, when it comes to relationships can barely boil a kettle.'

My *crème brûlée* was perfect, just nicely burnt on the top.

Matthew's secretary, at another table with her family, came over, put a hand on my shoulder and said in a stage whisper, 'Lucky girl. All I get is being sent to the post office.'

Matthew's phone rang.

An Algerian social sciences post-graduate, Galène Badda, had broken into his study and tried to light a fire there. Matthew relayed the story to us. 'When the fire-alarm went off, that old night-porter Harry charged into action. He turned a dry-powder fire extinguisher onto some smouldering paper, then onto this arsonist.'

'Lucky the paintings are not there,' I remarked.

'She's been taken to hospital with breathing difficulties.'

The coffees arrived with a dish of chocolates.

'Imogen, should you take your paintings up to Whitehaven?'

'I was just thinking the same.'

'Clare has plenty of spare room.'

Imogen explained that Matthew owned this spacious flat in Whitehaven. 'It's modern, second-floor, overlooks the marina and is rented out to Clare, his cousin.'

We dropped her in Ferry Pool Road and then ended our journey outside Matthew's flat in Canterbury Road.

After I had climbed out of the back seat of his old Saab, I thanked him for the exceptional meal, gave him a peck on his rather flabby cheek and – as he went in through his gateway – turned towards my old Polo. As I unlocked it, Lucinda's sports car drew into her driveway.

Its lights faded, she jumped out and marched out onto the pavement. 'Did *you* give those Kyoto museum booklets to Dusty?'

'Er, yes.'

One had been about medieval Japanese sword-smiths and the second a brief history of both cotton and silk kimonos.

'Well I've taken them from her. We don't want to learn about *swords*. So *don't* give her any more.' She stormed off into her house.

As P.G. Wodehouse puts it, 'Life never gives you a bit of goose without following it with a thwack in the windpipe.'

*   *   *   *

I woke up in the middle of a dream.

I had been in The Hanging Gardens of Babylon. This great ziggurat built of baked clay bricks – mostly pale yellow but with grey quoins and red-orange patterned gateways and arches – was filled with townsfolk, stairs, pools, date-palms, eucalyptus trees, shops and flowers. On the surrounding plain were fields and irrigation canals, farmers with ploughs and girls picking figs. The people had a sallow skin-colouring. They wore brown shifts or light loose ochre gowns. In the town were guards, priests, slaves, merchants, artisans, gardeners and dancing girls and up on the very top terrace, the priestess of al Lat – the sun goddess – outside her shrine, dressed in yellow and hung about with gold jewellery.

A unified civilisation.

I wondered what the priestess had said in her ancient babble?

Later I awoke again, this time in the middle of a nightmare.

I had shot three hikers.

Three wigged judges in splendid scarlet robes, shook their jowly heads and passed sentence on me for sedition and lawlessness. Some on the side benches exchanged satisfied smiles.

They left the court in chauffeur-driven limousines, unnamed establishment figures, untouchable, on huge salaries, with endless perks and enormous pension pots.

In the kitchen I made tea and nibbled a shortbread biscuit until I saw Stephanie's ghost, gave a shriek, fainted and hit my head on the table.

Alison must have heard. She came and propped me up, waited till I regained consciousness, then drank tea with me, but did not speak.

She guided me back to my bed.

CHAPTER TEN

The real gold nugget from Squibb's – from my point of view – starred Carole Grieff.

In Moreton-in-the-Marsh, I eyed the crooked Jacobean manor-house with its spiral brick chimneys. Its lowest course of stones consisted of large roughly-hewn cuboidal blocks half-buried in the ground. Foundations were not deep at that period. Above these were smaller and somewhat neater layers of stonework, which – according to the lintel – had been laid in 1609.

No one answered the door, but as I turned to go, a taxi drew up and a rather flustered looking woman climbed out.

'Excuse me, are you Carole Grieff?'

'Yes?' she snapped.

'You wrote an article regarding a Late Latin story about a Roman warship's fight with a pirate vessel in the Dodecanese?'

'What about it?'

'It's been pirated – very appropriately – and published in a Continental history magazine.'

'Oh?' She looked at me to see if I were deranged, then said in a softer tone, 'Well then ... come in.'

The gnarled oak front door with its black square-headed bolts and black iron knocker creaked gently back on its crude black wrought-iron hinges.

In the kitchen, she asked who I was.

'Sophie Hughes. I do research for Dr Matthew Sleight in Exeter.'

'Indeed.'

'Your article's appeared in French under the name, "Professeur Sylvie Leroy, S.I.P. D.R.Y. G.I.N."'

'Unusual qualifications?'

'Sorry, I was being flippant, but they're close to that. This periodical's office is in Bobigny, near Paris.'

She indicated a high, dark-oak dining-chair which had a carved back and a cushion on it.

I sat down and took a file from my bag – already photocopied – and passed it to her. She perused its copied sheets for some minutes.

The huge stone fire-place had a blackened oak lintel, an old cast-iron fire-basket with orange marigolds and blue cornflowers in it and a battered blue and red shield and two rusty swords hung up above it.

'Would you like a cup of tea?'

'Yes please.'

She switched the kettle on. 'Forgive my being a bit sharp. I've a new car, which instead of four simple coil springs – which never go wrong – has some elaborate and trouble-prone "compressed air" suspension.'

'Oh. You're not transporting Ming vases?'

'You hardly dare go ten miles from a main dealer with it.'

I tried to look sympathetic.

She found some scones and placed them on the dark-oak, marked and cup-stained Stuart-era table. Everything here looked period, except for the kettle, the modern china mugs and the plates.

'May I ask, how did you come by this material?'

'Another lecturer has been similarly defrauded ... and in looking into it, I unearthed this too.'

She looked at me a little uncertainly. 'That's a rather incomplete explanation?'

I did not answer.

She started to spread jam and cream on a scone, but stopped. 'I am none the less, grateful to you Sophie.'

'I ask you not to say that I was its source.'

'Very well. I will not do that.'

'Thank you. Say it came anonymously. That will actually be safer for both of us.'

We sipped our teas and bit into our scones. She had now calmed down.

'This is a very impressive home ... a bit like those Dutch seventeenth-century paintings with the dark dresser, the white walls and braided red and green draperies?'

She gave an unexpectedly friendly smile. 'We've made quite an effort over the years to collect genuine artefacts ... and I love the Stuart period ... the Restoration theatre, Purcell ... so much character.'

'The Civil War, the divine right of kings, the hocus-pocus of "the King's evil" can detract, but though the eighteenth century with its "enlightenment" seems more civilised, it is perhaps comparatively bland ... *too* refined ... or lacking in zeal?'

This off-the-cuff summary was intended to show that I was not a total half-wit ... or is that even less than a half-wit?

'As to this pilfered article, there's an odd slip – *haec signum* for *hoc signum* say – but it is my work. Did you do any Latin?'

'Only to G.C.S.E. My copy of *A Shorter Latin Primer* had had its cover title altered with a thick black felt-tip to *A Shorter way to eat Prime Beef*.'

Carole smiled briefly. 'As well as the outside of the property, that staircase has a conservation order on it.' She waved at a narrow skewed flight of elm back-stairs.

'Dr Grieff ... '

'Carole, please.'

'Carole, this play *The Eumenides* ... I couldn't have the part of Clytemnestra's Ghost, could I?'

Surprised by this, she hesitated. 'There are only nine named parts – the rest are Furies, Athenian citizens and such – and the standard is very high.'

'I understand.'

'That is a *very* big ask. Have you done much acting?'

'I was the sorceress in the film *A Surfeit of Devils* recently and in the summer I played a lot of small parts in a Welsh historical play, *Y Tywysog*, in Harlech Castle.'

She wanted a cigarette, so we went out into the walled back garden.

Dusk had started to fall and a number of lights – sunk into the ground alongside the path – suddenly lit up.

'Like an airfield?' I remarked.

'A very small one. So make sure you only come in your vertical-take-off-and-landing jet.'

'I'll remember that.'

'It won an "eco" award last year.'

'I would have thought any garden was "eco-friendly"?'

'Well, it won an award anyway.'

'My parents' garden has grass a foot high so it must be guzzling up the carbon dioxide ... but no one's given it an "eco" award.'

She laughed softly and stubbed out her cigarette.

'I am in your debt ... and Mervyn will give this lot hell

... ' She hesitated. 'But I will have to audition you first.'

'That's absolutely fine.' It seemed I had cut a teensy bit of ice.

'I will study these papers again later, but you're sure that "Clio" is Gavin O'Rourke?'

'There's no other possibility.'

'Gosh, how Oxford's changed. My grandfather was at Corpus Christi, the reader in Anglo-Norman ... he loved the medieval period.'

In contrast to her husband, there was no affectation in Carole; she was not overly 'professional'.

She showed me out by the side gate.

I rang Matthew.

'Matthew, you know that Mervyn chap, Imogen's enemy?'

'Yes?'

'Well, I think he's about to become your friend.'

'What?'

'He's about to fight a proxy war for you ... he'll be taking a very big stick to that chancer Gavin O'Rourke.'

*   *   *   *

In Station Road, Wylde Green, Birmingham, Eirig and I looked over the slightly rusty wrought-iron gates at the nineteen-thirties, semi-detached, mock-Tudor house. The blinds were drawn and its appearance – if not exhausted – was at least tired.

On the weed-dotted gravel stood the white Ford van whose number plate Megan had noted and whose details Roderick had looked up.

I took a photo of it.

A rough woman in her thirties appeared. 'What are you doing?'

I smiled pleasantly. 'I'm a private detective and this van was recently involved in an attempted robbery in Wales.'

'Well, it wasn't, because it's awaiting a rebore.'

'I see.'

'It's burning oil.'

'Oh, well then I can exclude it from my inquiries.'

During this exchange a man of similar age had come up behind the woman.

'No,' he addressed me, 'Vanessa is referring to another van. Jason – her brother – did borrow this van two weeks ago.'

I looked at him and – surprised by his honesty – said, 'Thank you. We'll pursue the matter no farther.'

Eirig and I walked away.

'Mercy' is often misunderstood. It is not simply letting someone off the hook, but offering a way out in return for some form of restitution or contrition.

Mostafa Khan – whose nose Dad had broken – was one of the gang who had attacked the Indians in Anson Street. He had received a non-custodial sentence of community work, because his cat had been poorly at the time and the need to care for it was apparently a 'human right'.

I now had the complete picture of the raid which Megan and Dad had thwarted.

'Megan's such a stalwart, Eirig. If only she could find a sensible boyfriend ... but her current obsession's taking her nowhere.'

*   *   *   *

The Ferry Pool Leisure Centre has a twenty-five metre pool and I had begun to go there when it was open for lane swimming.

I came out after thirty-three lengths into the sunshine and set off to walk the two miles back to the Annex, but as I turned the corner from Ferry Pool Road into Marston Ferry Road, I was surprised to see Luke Mpofu stood on the lawn, looking up at Imogen's balcony.

I called over. 'Hullo.'

He turned, smiled and came up to other side of the low hedge. 'Sophie?'

'Yes.'

'I've just rung Imogen's bell.'

'She's in Whitehaven.'

'Oh.'

'Why have you come to see her ... at home?'

He paused, then rather awkwardly said, 'I wondered if she would give me lessons?'

'I've not heard of her giving lessons.'

'No.'

'Someone tried to break-in back in June.' I wondered if he might know anything about this. 'She's had a mortise lock fitted into her flat's main door to supplement the cylinder lock.'

'So a burglar would need a ladder to climb up to the balcony?'

'Yes ... but she keeps a pot of boiling pitch on the stove ... just in case.'

He nodded as if this were a serious remark. 'Will you keep a secret?'

'Yes.'

'I sent her the tip-off.'

I inhaled slowly and thought – as in cartoon balloons – '@&€*%!!!'

'I overheard Datir discussing it with some detective agency guy.'

'Goodness. We owe you then, a very serious thank you.'

'You mustn't say anything.'

'I won't. I promise ... except to Imogen ... if that's all right?'

'Yes.'

'Who was the intruder?'

'I don't have a name.'

'I thought it might be someone from a Pakistani take-away ... but this guy was white.'

'A take-away?'

'Why do you want lessons?'

'I was given the junior lectureship here because I had worked for an art investigation bureau in London and learnt a lot about pigments – old, natural and synthetic – plant dyes, minerals, canvas types, customs stamps, brush hairs, varnish and so on ... and that's quite a big field now.'

I nodded gently.

'Art can do so much for the soul ... and I so want to improve.'

'But do you think that painting, perhaps – as with musical composition – is more of a gift than a result of effort?'

'Not entirely.'

'Churchill took lessons from leading artists and worked extremely hard at his paintings ... yet the results are no more than average.' I paused. 'That break-in? What was the plan?'

'I'm not sure. Damage perhaps ... or theft?'

'It's almost beyond belief.'

There was a break in the dialogue.

'Why did you suggest a take-away?'

'A local take-away rents out thugs ... but I suppose lock-picking is more specialised?'

'I love living here. I'm very lucky.'

'Good. You're a good man ... you deserve some happiness.'

'Dr Eze's in my college. He says that as a coloured person it's my job to fight, to rebel, to demand respect ... but I don't see it like that.'

'Arrogance is not a good path ... that's for sure.'

'For this information, do you think Imogen might give me one of her paintings?'

I grinned. 'I would think so.' My grin broadened. 'What about that space-ship picture ... blues, greys and three green Martians with aerials on their heads?'

He smiled. 'It's quite comical. With its economy of strokes and its odd touches, it's almost in a cartoon-like style.'

I gave him a friendly farewell.

'I'll see you around.'

I decided to catch a bus into town and on it, thought about Stephanie, about loyalty and trust. Certainly governmental institutions were becoming less and less trustworthy.

A fellow in the supermarket at Stroud had stopped Eirig and quite seriously asked to buy Ceinlys. Either with this doll or with a dog you were very fond of, if someone offered you a lot of money and you accepted, you would diminish your soul by such a betrayal.

In most ancient societies, loyalty and belonging were everything; money a mere side-show.

Later in the Annex, Libby answered the door-bell, then climbed the stairs with a Manilla envelope.

'For me?'

A sheet of sugar paper bore a crude sketch of a girl – with a squeezed tube of paint in one hand – hanging from a gibbet with her neck broken, as indicated by her head hanging to one side. Under it lay written with the same blunt 4B pencil, 'I.S.' A second attached scrap of paper had a note on it in a different hand. 'The enclosed was doodled by Dr Raju Datir, June the second. L.M.'

Tyrants are not open to negotiation, but hardened and relentless. The corporal in Jerusalem was right to shoot the Arab. Had he shown leniency the bomber would simply have thought him a fool and gone off to throw more grenades. Mercy had no *rôle* to play in that scenario.

I posted Dr Datir's doodle on the Art Faculty's website with the caption, 'A cartoon by Dr Raju Datir.'

Before bed I dipped into Libby's book on Zeno. It was concise; always a good start.

Happiness, he states in his book *On Nature*, can only be obtained by a steady flow of good deeds and true friendships, all leavened with self-discipline, integrity and coherent thought.

So keep a clear mind, avoid over-thinking everything, do not over-react, do not complain about your lot. Being truthful will only lose for you the friends who never were friends.

The last book I had been lent had been pretentious. It had had spurious poetic bits, where odd letters were alone on lines. 'I only read as far as page ten,' I had said, when returning it.

'Oh,' said its owner, 'But it doesn't start till page eleven?'

By ten the next morning, Dr Datir's cartoon had received forty-six hits. By ten thirty, it had been taken down and my permission to post, blocked.

*   *   *   *

The coroner's inquest into Stephanie's death had opened.

Dr Jobling, a pathologist near to retirement – his skin made pale and waxy by its years of exposure to formalin vapour – had been the first to give evidence.

The deceased, he related, had always been in good health, her only medical record being of a tonsillectomy when six.

Engrossed, I knelt on a kitchen chair with the paper spread out on the table. I could half imagine the sixty-three-year-old in his orangey-brown rubber apron with Stephanie's naked body on his slab.

Jobling had said how the slight but unusual bruising around the angles of her jaw had led him to a careful search inside her mouth and there, under her tongue, he had found a small blood blister, most likely caused by a needle puncture.

Slicing the heart and brain had revealed no cardiac or cerebral lesions. Her stomach had contained no residue of the pills as labelled on the empty bottles found beside her body. Jobling had then conjectured that insulin had been forcibly injected, leading to hypoglycaemia, coma and death.

The Coroner, Richard Plantagenet Johns – his father had been an admirer of Richard the Third – had further probed this unexpected finding.

Jobling explained that since insulin cannot be administered orally, there had to be a puncture wound if it had indeed been given.

Madge Wells – a lady who lived in the village – had walked her dog Coco past Stephanie's cottage the previous evening. Stephanie had been in her garden and they had exchanged a few pleasant words. Stephanie had seemed to be her usual cheerful self.

Stephanie's brother Gerard also told the court that his sister was not someone who would commit suicide, nor had any recent events in her life led her to be unduly anxious.

Madge Wells' husband, a local journalist, was in the public gallery and feeling instinctively that the pill bottles were indeed a ruse, he raised the possibility of foul play in a small three paragraph article written for his paper's morning edition the following day.

After tea, on searching the internet, he discovered that in 1934, one Thomas Birch had chosen the fold of the left gluteal sulcus as his insulin injection site, when murdering a lover who was trying to blackmail him. He too had chosen a spot where he did not expect the pathologist to look, though was similarly unlucky. He ended up on the scaffold.

Wells rang Steve Duckett, a reporter friend in London and they wrote a joint article for the national paper for which Duckett worked. The editor thought it engaging enough to slot in on page six.

Day two of this inquest was preparing to start at ten o'clock when it was halted by the Department of Justice in London. Instead an 'inquiry into Stephanie Norman's suicide' would be substituted, in London and *in camera*. The reason given was that she worked in intelligence.

The cause of death was thus pre-determined and all press coverage banned, the facts being labelled *sub judice*.

CHAPTER ELEVEN

Imogen asked me to go with her to a summons from some inter-collegiate diversity and equality board, but wanted first to drive to Abingdon.

'You need someone with you ... if only as a witness.'

'I had a visit from a Deborah Chatiswa, Luke's partner. She came to collect *The Martians*, which I had promised her husband. She comes from Zambia. I gave her tea. She's quite petite, very unassuming ... and works in a nursery in Witney.'

'At least you have a spy in the enemy camp.'

'How's the sheep book going?'

'Apparently there are two animals which easily just give up and die; sheep and Siamese cats ... but why are we going to Abingdon?'

She found a piece of paper. 'This was under my nose, but I only realised it two days since. The "parcel" which that burglar had, the one who tried to break in in June, was just an empty box.'

'Left behind in the kerfuffle?'

'Inside though was this delivery note. It's to; "Graves Private Investigators".'

'In Abingdon?'

'Yes.'

'I heard of a guy who wanted to know if a certain girl had a boyfriend. The detective agency charged him for camping outside her flat for a week with a camera, when what they actually did was ring her door-bell and pretend to be selling cheaper electricity tariffs. One of them then faked a heart attack, so they gained access and noted the bedding arrangements.'

We parked in Ock Street and found the small glass-fronted office.

A tall young man in a white shirt and a blue tie sat at a desk.

We went in and photographed him.

'What are you doing?'

'You're the man who tried to break in to Imogen's flat here in June.'

I glimpsed a fibre-optic cable and its light-source boxed-up to one side, something which could be slid snake-like under a door.

We left before he could throw any brick-bats.

In Oxford, the architects of our sterile new world kept us waiting, probably to impress upon us how busy they were with more urgent matters.

It was a hot day and Dr Eze, the large Ghanaian, glistened with beads of sweat. His eye-balls protruded a little and seemed to swivel very noticeably.

'Sit down,' he commanded us gruffly.

His eye-balls bulged even more on recognising me.

'Imogen, could we speak alone?'

'The rules say you can bring a friend?'

'Very well,' he growled. 'Firstly, how do you identify?'

'Umm ... Imogen Rachael Sleight?'

'I'm referring to orientation ... sex, religion, race.'

She frowned. 'Umm ... I'm a sheep. Rachael means "sheep" ... a Llanwenog.'

'How do you spell that?' He jotted down her answer. 'The rules are that we now have to ask this.'

'Oh.'

'As the Deconstructing Whiteness Officer, a concern has been brought to me by two of your lecturers.'

'Oh?'

'They say that you only paint white people?'

'Not true ... some are Biblical or Near-Eastern ... oh and three were green.'

'But no black people?'

'Er ... probably not.'

They say that your style is basically neo-classical ... that you're simply replicating others ... that there's nothing new?'

'My style is not neo-classical. It's simpler and less intense.'

Eze leaned forwards and bent to his real purpose

'To head off a discriminatory hearing, it has been suggested that you paint a large canvas of some asylum seekers coming ashore ... they would be of mixed race? Imagine ... the spray, the gulls?'

Imogen's eyes widened. 'I can only paint if I feel my Muse is telling me to ... or at least if it is something which engages me.'

'But think ... a new venture ... we are all works in progress?'

I was tempted to ask when he had thought of starting?

He leant back. 'My college has applied for a government grant to replace some of the lead on the chapel roof.'

'Oh.'

'The grant is available, but is conditional on a display about sanctuary and asylum being set up at the west end of the chapel for five years. If you were to contribute such ... it would be enormously appreciated.'

I knew Imogen would never yield. 'This is state-sponsored propaganda. It's undemocratic. It's like the old Eastern Europe.'

Imogen added, 'Would it not be better for your college to maintain its integrity and patch up any leaks as best it can?'

There was a hiatus.

'An American came to the Department, looking for you. What did he want?'

'Oh ... he bought one of my paintings for The National Gallery in Washington. Twenty thousand dollars.'

After a deep breath came, 'The Reverend Elaine-Marie Gooch, our vice-chair, suggested this meeting to try to resolve this matter.'

The word 'vice' sounded very apt, in many ways.

'It shows good-will on her part.'

'Or a test, to see if Imogen will bow to your idols?' I suggested.

'Perhaps you should reciprocate?'

Imogen showed him the photo on her phone of the fellow at Abingdon. 'Dr Datir – no doubt one of those behind this meeting – arranged for this man to break into my flat in June.'

'What?'

'We have evidence and could go to the police.'

The meeting ended in mid-air.

We stopped on the Magdalen bridge and peered down at the punts.

'There are civilisations which have declined ... through decadence or through losing their trade or their genius ... but none before have deliberately cut their own throats.'

'True.'

On the river two punts – a green one and an orange one – bumped each other.

'That picture ... I thought you said five thousand dollars?'

'I did. The twenty was just to wind him up.'

'You could have said it was the fee for copying a Cannelloni.'

'True ... but he wrote on scrolls, didn't he?'

The sky was cloudless, the air warm. 'What a lovely day ... and those quiet drooping willow trees?'

I smiled amicably at those enjoying picnics on the river bank.

I was surprised that Megan had not asked, 'Has anyone taken a punt on you yet?'

*   *   *   *

Eirig thumbed through *The Eumenides*.

'The current quip is that it's "Zeus-less",' I said.

'Does Zeus not appear in it?'

'No.'

'And Clytemnestra's Ghost has just this one forty-two line speech?'

'Yes.'

'And that's the part you want?'

'Yes. Orestes, her son, has killed her because she killed his father, her husband, Agamemnon. Her excuse is that Agamemnon had sacrificed their daughter Iphigenia to obtain a favourable wind at Aulis, to blow the fleet to Troy. It was in reality though because she had a lover, Aegisthus. None the less, the Furies are taking Clytemnestra's side, because a mother-murder is by ancient lore they say, an unforgiveable sin.'

'An austere coven?'

'It nearly didn't happen I've learnt. The committee which usually finances the society insisted that some of the Furies be dressed as refugees and some extra lines of their own invention be inserted ... but a Greek businessman stepped in, much to the chagrin of those "high-minded" narcissists.' I thought, then added, 'An odd thing about narcissists is that they lose the ability to love.'

'And then today often hide behind a gilded morality?'

We were sat side by side. He put his arm round my shoulders and murmured, 'I'll tell you something.'

I knitted my brows and whispered humorously, 'Is it intimate?'.

'Very. The girls I have taken out before you, have always been hard ... wanting to use me. Also I have no sister ... and this has tempted me at times into unkind thoughts about your sex.'

'Surely not?'

'Ceinlys has been an antidote. I cuddle her and she dispels anything dark or grim.'

'I wonder how many psychiatrists would recommend a doll as therapy?'

'We're all different.'

I gave a perplexed smile, cuddled him and we went to bed.

On the morrow, at Matthew's, the ground-floor tenant was just leaving. She said to her two toddlers, 'Yes I know, my little sillies ... I know you want cuddles.' This gave me a twinge of pain; an intimacy I would never know.

Eating cake with your coffee is – Matthew said – quite a

Scandinavian custom and today it was walnut cake.

'Matthew, is there any reason why O'Rourke should bear a grudge against Carole Grieff?'

'Umm ... she voted against his election to his current post.'

'That sounds a rather petty reason.'

'True, but he's good at being petty. She was on the interview panel, which he attended in a yellow suede jacket and afterwards referred to him as a "lemon puff." I learnt recently that one reference was from a Doctor Axel Lindström in Minnesota. Now many Scandinavians did settle there, so that seemed credible, but it included too an accolade from a "Jørgen Hattemaker".'

'Oh.'

'This name translates as "George Hatter" but it is the Nordic equivalent of "Fred Bloggs".'

'So just "Mr Anybody"?'

'And there was a second fake commendation from a "Herr Økseskaft". This name means "Mr Axe-handle", but it isn't a real name. It's just used to describe someone who's dense or slow on the uptake.'

'Hmm. I'll send a note to Mervyn. He's good at sarcasm. He might be able to weave some of this into his cross-questioning.'

'Mervyn's been interviewed recently by a Metropolitan police commissioner and an officer from the Garda.'

'Oh.'

A mischievous twinkle came into Matthew's eye. 'It's lucky he's not an electrician.'

I thought for a few moments. 'Ah ... because he wouldn't be able to reach the fuse-box?'

We both laughed.

*　　*　　*　　*

At home I asked Dad, who had served in Northern Ireland, if he had heard of any bullion robberies south of the border.

'Er ... one.'

'When?'

'Seven or eight years back?'

'Did it succeed?'

'Yes, but one of the gang nearly died.'

'Oh?'

'Some R.E.M.E. lads had found a rifle belonging to the I.R.A. They took it to their workshop where they drilled a criss-cross of vertical holes down into the left-hand wall of the firing-chamber, before sealing them over. They then replaced it ... and it blew up in the face of the first Provo to pull the trigger.'

'You mustn't repeat that to anyone!'

'It could have saved an innocent person's life.'

'None the less, in today's world, do *not* repeat it. We don't want fifty human rights lawyers banging on the door.'

'Sophie, "tact" is my middle name.'

Was this humour which is so poor as to be good? I could not contort my face sufficiently. 'Pardon?' I put a finger in my ear and wiggled it.

'You cheeky piccaninny.'

Megan came in. She had finally had a *cappuccino* with Daryl – alias Romeo – where he had demonstrated his 'Bull-worker'.

This 'Bull-worker' was a set of five long tension springs with hand-grips at each end, which you could expand and release across your chest to develop your arm muscles.

'He stretched it quite impressively, but as he relaxed it, all his pectoral hairs became trapped in the springs and ... ' She lay down on the sofa, paralysed, scarcely able to breathe and with tears in her eyes.

'I suggest you trade him in for a new model ... one that goes.'

Being fair-haired and nicely rounded in the right places, I am often not without admirers, but lovers are different. You cannot conjure them out of thin air.

Over lunch Megan asked, 'So this "Sweetie Pie", this secret boyfriend of yours, what model is *it*?'

'If it rattles a bit, who cares? Opulence is decadence.'

'So ... vintage or veteran, steam or pulled by oxen?'

I gave her a shake of the head. 'The day is young.'

'It's not that young.'

I could see this was not going to end. 'If you must know, it's Eirig.'

'Our cousin?'

'Yes.'

Mum looked at me. 'You can't marry a first cousin? It's incest?'

'Not in Britain.'

Megan chewed it over. 'Hmm, it's not easy to get it right, is it?'

I glanced at her. 'It's easy to get it wrong ... for some of us.'

Mum, Dad and Megan drove off to Caernarfon.

The Stephanie Norman Inquiry, despite being *in camera*, was arousing a lot of interest. Everyone scented treachery.

A police commissioner – an array of medals on his chest – had been filmed arriving, though given his lack of involvement, his presence was seemingly mere window-dressing.

A micro-biology professor spoke of cocco-bacilli growing on his agar plates – stained pink and purple – from Stephanie's nasopharynx, as possible evidence of a sudden, highly virulent and lethal infection. No one bought that either.

Coroner Richard Johns, although gagged by a high-court injunction, quoted Jonathan Swift to a posse of journalists; 'The law is a net which catches midges whilst allowing wasps and hornets to sail straight through.'

I had printed off the photos, left them in Eirwen's unknowing care and deleted the originals from my phone.

Uncle Hywel called and mentioned that *The Simple Milkmaid* had closed. 'It's going to be an Italian eatery, *Sophie's Siesta Palace.*'

'Oh, that sounds promising.' I told him of the take-away in Anson Street in Oxford.

Had the attack on Judith come from one of its ruffians, either contracted or just impulsive?

Hywel had been a policeman back in the seventies. 'After our training, we took an oath before a stipendiary magistrate – I believe they're now called district judges – and it included the phrase "to act without fear or favour".'

I made tea and found some doughnuts.

'How are your Oxford skirmishes going?'

'Quite well ... but we're not rushing our fences ... playing a long game.'

Some custard dripped onto his woolly, which he scraped off with an index finger. 'I'm changing my will. If you add a codicil, then when published, the original can still be seen, so I'm rewriting it from scratch.'

'But the codicil would chasten anyone who had annoyed you by revealing their loss?' I thought this mildly amusing, but Uncle Hywel is a serious fellow.

'My old theological college is now scrubbed. Its scholarships and bursaries are all donated by the white middle-class ... a group now side-lined and dismissed.'

Hywel had been in the Territorials, in an artillery regiment.

'The brass cartridge cases of our twenty-five pounders contained cordite in three canvas bags, red white and blue. For 'low charge' you left only the red bag in, for 'medium' the red and the white and for 'high' all three. The left-over bags of propellant you laid end-to-end afterwards and lit one end with a match. They burnt briskly but did not explode. The increase of pressure in the barrel – and so behind the shell – has to be gradual.'

An analogy perhaps as to how to fight psychological battles.

CHAPTER TWELVE

Carole Grieff asked me round and – with a slight agitation beneath her customary cool demeanour – spoke initially of her article.

'I've early dated versions, so in accusing Squibb's of a breach of copyright, we have a rock solid case ... and the letters you copied prove the link between them and this Sylvie Leroy and her editor.'

We were drinking tea and eating toast in her kitchen.

She had sent it to *Classical Sites Today*, one of Squibb's educational journals. 'The letter signed by Lacey to the French journal's editor stated, "Herewith the required 'original' of Dr Grieff's letter, giving her permission for her article to be translated and sold on."'

She put more bread in the toaster.

'I liked the line, "The Roman ship had blue-dyed sails and rigging for camouflage." It makes it more alive.'

Carole ignored this. 'This letter has my forged signature and a hand-written postscript. Mervyn has a book on forgery. These efforts just look ponderous. My minuscule 'm's have a distinctively long arch between the first and second vertical strokes, but a mere spike between the second and third ... and curved serifs on the 't's.

The density of the ink shows it is being written slowly and the smoother, more widely spaced letters imply more hand and wrist movement. I use mostly finger movements, giving a more cramped or pointed style. The final down-stroke of his rounded 'a' does not retrace the up-stroke but deviates to the right of it. His 'l's and 'h's are formed with loops, which are seldom narrow enough to become filled-in and there's an eyelet on top of a capital 'J'. Lastly I break before the letters 'a', 'o' and 'g', which the forger has not replicated.'

'You've spent time on this.'

'They were not expecting it to be scrutinised.'

'And the forger?'

'It's Lacey. His hand-writing is on that page copied from the address book, a couple of marginal notes and his signature.'

'So you have them by the short and curlies?'

'It looks that way.' She poured more tea. 'Sophie, to move on to *The Eumenides* ... '

'Can I recite Clytemnestra's speech? I've learnt it off by heart.'

She smiled faintly and waved a nonchalant hand, so I stood up and did – I thought – a good rendition, imagining myself amid the dozing somnolent Furies, being mildly sarcastic in places and varying my speech between softer tones and more abrasive ones.

Carole smiled to herself. 'When you said "chest", you thrust your left shoulder forwards. Perhaps you should open an anatomy book?'

I had an uneasy feeling and it proved justified.

'Sophie, I'm under a lot of pressure ... how would you feel about a part in the chorus?'

If Carole had already chosen someone, I had to persuade her to 'unchoose' her. I cannot explain it, but I so desperately wanted this part. 'You said that if I was competent enough, you would let me have this?'

She gave an odd squint which lasted for some seconds.

'Sophie, you can have it. I did promise. I'm sorry.'

'Thank you,' I replied with relief. 'If I lack depth or character, you can recommend a drama teacher. I'm prepared to make an effort.'

She buttered more toast.

I took a photograph from my bag. 'I was about to show you this.'

'Oh? 'Northumberland?'

'The note given to Mervyn had the wrong grid reference on it.'

'Oh?'

'And the orange sports car gave him away.'

She squeezed out a thin smile. 'I told him to use our son's jalopy ... but he's obsessed with the Lotus.'

Psychologists call such cars 'penile extensions', which I do not really understand.

'Sophie if I tell you something in confidence ... will you promise that it will go no further?'

'Yes.'

'Mervyn and I are planning to separate?'

'I have not heard that.'

'He wants to retire to the South of France with his new girlfriend ... and the plan is that I keep the house, my own pension and a third of our investments.'

I nodded. 'Well at least you've agreed a plan?'

'He very unwisely involved himself with a corrupt police officer who knew about some stolen precious metals. There was an unexpected gang fight and a murder ... which left only one survivor who knew where these wretched baubles were hidden.'

'Yes,' I said, as if I already knew this.

'At first they thought the killer was Chinese, but that was a ruse. Both gangs were Indian and the killer – Pradesh Pathak – was sent down for twenty-two years. Recently he gave the location in exchange for a lump sum to be paid to his family ... and was then tortured and murdered in Wormwood Scrubs by fellow inmates, when the location turned out to be wrong.'

I asked, 'You have enough money between you surely, so why involve yourselves in this ... grubby stuff?'

'I agree with you entirely ... but he wants to give up law and retire with this hussy ... in luxury.'

'I've just spent a holiday in France, where I helped a local builder retile an old barn. You need *some* money but not mountains of it.'

'That sounds more attractive than some tacky villa.'

'I could get him into trouble ... but I won't.'

Again she gave me a long penetrating look which ended with a droll smile.

She wrote down the name and telephone number of a drama teacher. 'I'll tell her you're coming and explain the part she's to work on. She's a bit airs-and-graces, but bear with it ... she's very intuitive.'

As I left she gave me a curious but friendly nod.

In the Annex, I flopped onto my bed and felt oddly satisfied.

I had avoided using say a variant of Henry Ford's Model T remark; 'You can have anyone you want, so long as it's *me*.' All had worked out well. Shaw once said, 'You create your own opportunities.'

Then, as I thought about her odd smiles, I suddenly understood. She sensed that I had some link with the intelligence world ... and so no doubt did she.

*   *   *   *

I could not attend Stephanie's funeral because of anonymous eyes in dark suits, but I visited Judith soon afterwards.

The inquiry had ended, its pre-determined conclusions published in a three-hundred page document.

Judith had been allowed to attend one session.

'A permanent under-secretary – Ponsford Button – claimed that Stephanie had betrayed secrets to "foreign powers" and suggested that her taking her own life had most likely been due to her unwillingness to face up to her crimes.'

'A line no outsider could prove or disprove?'

'Because of their "sensitivity", he could "reveal no details".'

Judith uncorked some fizzy wine. It popped.

She poured out two glasses. 'To Stephanie.'

'My Uncle Hywel preaches that in heaven, there will be no lies or smooth talking.'

'Time might throw something up.'

'Let's hope so ... and then Stephanie can rest in peace?'

Judith had already boxed up most of their belongings. 'I'm leaving on Friday.'

We exchanged contact details and as I left, I gave her a hug.

In the upstairs kitchen in the Annex, a book belonging to Emma lay open. She had returned from Italy.

I read; 'The fair land of Canaan had extensive cedar forests, snow on its mountains and grapes in its vineyards. Its rocky gorges and wooded groves were enchanted, inhabited by local deities. In the coastal ports the rare purple dye – extracted from the murex seashells – was purified for the robes of kings ... '

The door-bell rang.

A white male, tall, well-dressed and well-schooled in a decidedly supercilious manner, stood on the step.

'I'm looking for an S. I. Hughes.'

'And who are you?'

He produced a laminated official-looking identity card headed 'Ministry of Information' which included amongst other bogus details, his name.

'Well I'm Sophie Hughes.'

'Oh ... you're a girl?' He pronounced the word 'girl' with curled lips and evident distaste.

'It would appear so.'

'May I ask a few questions?'

'So you've decided to give up on duff police sergeants?'

He pretended not to have heard this. 'May I come in?'

'No.'

In an irritated tone, he asked, 'Does the acronym STUB mean anything to you?'

'No ... but by all means unravel it.'

His smile was one of condescension; guarded, prickly. 'I'm not sure that anyone actually knows. "Saboteurs to undo Britain" has been suggested ... but with no firm basis.'

'Oh.'

'However, there's a suspicion that you have distributed information about their ordering of brochures?'

'Oh? Then why was Stephanie Norman murdered?'

He angled his eyebrows in simulated bemusement.

'By two men and a woman?'

He rocked his head from side to side.

'All clearly photographed.'

He had not expected this. 'There are things called court injunctions.'

'They can be circumnavigated.'

'Hmm ... I will have to discuss this with my chief.'

'Good.' I went in and closed the door.

Alison appeared and warmed up a bowl of what was seemingly her sole recipe of salami chunks, tomatoes and onions.

'Tea?' I asked.

'No thank you.'

I boiled the kettle.

'I hear you've been given a part in *The Eumenides*?'

'Yes. I was very lucky.'

'Carolyn French was quite miffed. She's won lots of drama awards – two at national level – and felt herself well-fitted to that part.'

'Oh?'

There was both hostility and suspicion in her tone.

'Anyway, this bowl of salami and lentils might restore me to my usual humour.'

I hoped this would be an improvement rather than a worsening of its current level.

Trying to steer onto safer ground, I said, 'It's usually played in a very stern or dour way ... yet there are patches where a bit of humour might be possible?'

She looked at me.

'I can see myself prodding these semi-comatose Furies, these snoring lumps of flesh and being quite facetious.'

'It can't be treated *too* flippantly,' came her staid riposte. 'With Aeschylus, the religious element is still sincere.'

'Well, we'll see how Carole wants to do it? Are you in it?'

'In the Chorus of Athenian Citizens.'

'Oh. Good.' I exited on tip-toe, stage left, to my room.

I typed, 'Silver and platinum ingots.'

A murder had occurred, I discovered, in 2012 near Kirknewton, between Coldstream and Wooler, tenuously linked via a fence in London to the Galway precious metals' robbery. The head of the dead man – one Ashok Balaji – had been battered, his scrotum cut open and its contents stuffed into his mouth, before a very heavy log had been dropped across his face. Such victim mutilation was known – it stated – to be an old Chinese practice.

Deciding that the coast was clear, I crept back to the kitchen to heat up a fish pie.

Emma appeared simultaneously, looking quite distraught, her eyes red.

'Hullo Emma.'

She said nothing.

I sensed that if I said more, she might burst into tears.

As I turned on the oven, she took a glass pot of goulash out of the fridge and put it on an oven-glove on the table. This then caught on her sleeve button, which dragged the bowl with it, causing it to crash onto the floor and break.

She burst into jerky sobs.

I helped to clear it up. 'Are you not going to salvage some and eat it?'

'No. The glass has splintered. It would be too risky.'

'You can share my fish pie, it's quite large ... and I've a couple of rolls ... though with a bit of mould on them. It'll only be penicillium, which won't harm us.'

She dried her eyes, sat on one of the high stools at the table and watched with a rigid face, as I set these rolls out with some butter and made tea.

'Has something happened?' I asked.

She put her elbows on the table and rested her forehead in her hands.

Had she done something wrong? And if so, was a touch of self-worth now troubling her?

'Are you still seeing Professor O'Rourke?'

'No. That finished. There's something odd about his smile. His face smiles but not his eyes. They're flat. Like a cod's.'

'Oh?'

'I feel so ... restless.'

I waited.

'It started at a party. I was drunk. He put an arm round me and I put a hand down his trousers and fumbled his bits. Heaven knows why? He said, "I didn't realise you were a Freemason?" I giggled and off we went to his house.'

I checked the progress of the fish pie. 'Someone called Duncan came to see you.'

'O'Rourke arranged to have my tuition fees paid by a college donor.'

'A donor?'

'An Arab living in Abu Dhabi ... who wants his son to come to Oxford.'

The kitchen window was propped open and outside two youths were kicking a fizzy drinks tin around and swearing. I closed it.

With an embroidered handkerchief pulled out of the cuff of her cardigan, Emma gave her eyes a final dab.

'Is refusing Duncan the reason why things don't work out?'

She spread a knob of butter on a bisected roll, then nodded lamely.

The oven pinged and I scooped the fish pie onto two plates after warming them in hot water.

Changing tack, I asked if she had ever had lectures from Simon Cummings.

'Yes. He's excellent ... very colourful.'

'I hear he was thrown out of the church?'

'He'd been quite critical of their obsessions with climate change and transgender issues, saying that prayer should be more mystical and less secular.'

I dusted the thickest cluster of bluey-green fungal fibres from another roll and placed two mugs of tea on the table.

'Then he played an April fools' gag on his bishop's boyfriend, who was supplying drugs to a night-club owner named Mona Subic. When he told him that she had been arrested for selling on his opioids, this boyfriend panicked and swilled his eighteen-thousand-pound stash down the plug-hole.'

'And then discovered it to be a hoax?'

'He went crazy and started denting Simon's car with a lump hammer until Simon came out with a shovel and knocked him senseless.'

'And the bishop took his boyfriend's side?'

'Naturally.'

'"Colourful" is definitely the right adjective. I imagine the press lapped it up?'

'They were as happy as sand-boys.'

'And was the bishop pleased?'

'He was thrilled ... at least in so far as getting rid of Simon.'

We ate for a time in silence. I thought of Duncan ... and Eirig. Although God teases us about many things, He does not do so about love.

I put our plates in the sink, then cast a glance at her. 'At least the fish pie has brightened you up?'

She managed a smile.

'Does Professor O'Rourke have a "friend" who's a South African cricket umpire?'

'Not that I know of. He has a boyfriend. There's a photo of him on his bedside table.'

'Oh. What's his name?'

'I asked that, but he ignored the question. In the picture he has a book open and face-down on his thigh. You can just make out the title ... and it's in Russian.'

'Oh.'

'He looks Slavic ... big ears and a flabby face.'

'He has powerful supporters ... this king of the castle?'

Emma offered to do the washing-up, so I thanked her and rose to go back to my room.

She whispered, 'He lives in Christ Church.'

'What the Russian?'

'No. Duncan.'

*   *   *   *

I had agreed to meet Imogen for afternoon tea.

In Broad Street we watched a scuffle.

A physics student had explained to a class-mate why we always see the same side of the moon. Its centre of gravity is off-set, so it behaves like a ball of uneven density, which will always settle denser-side down on a flat surface.

The dialogue had then touched on the American moon landings which some passing Moslems stopped to dispute. The moon is quite sacred to their religion and the idea that the Americans had landed there was to them both offensive and profane.

The violence was not too serious, but punches were being thrown. Four police officers nearby watched, but remained immobile.

We realised that we were stood beside the cross outside Balliol College, formed on the ground by granite cobbles. It marks the position of the stake at which Cranmer, Ridley and Latimer had been burnt under Bloody Mary.

'The writing's on the wall,' I remarked, 'and it does not need Daniel to interpret it.'

'I wonder how long before we shall again see Christians being martyred in England?'

Over cauliflower and Stilton soup Imogen said, 'Matthew says that the investigation into Elaine-Marie Gooch's selling on the Margaret Taylor article ended with "N.F.A." scrawled on the front of the file.'

'What's "N.F.A."?'

'No further action.'

'Oh.'

'Her defence was that she eats Smarties and it has been shown that the colouring used for the yellow ones causes hyperactivity and attention deficit, so these sweets were – she pleaded – a mitigating factor in her confusion.'

'That sounds convincing.'

'Matthew's taking a holiday in Sweden, in Mariefred. It's beside a lake and has a narrow gauge railway and a castle. You can buy waffles with jam and cream from a kiosk near the band-stand.'

'It sounds lovely.'

Imogen asked about Welsh orthography and in particular its eight double-letter consonants.

'I believe they came about when printing presses came into use. As the type was all Roman, they had to find ways to express Welsh sounds using only the letters available in the type boxes.'

'So before that were there other hand-written symbols for those sounds?'

'I suppose so ... but I don't know what they looked like.'

She wanted me to come back with her to her flat, where she took out a carrot cake and made coffee.

'Sophie, there's a ruined Crusader castle in northern Israel, Belvoir ... a little south of Lake Galilee. It's on a high ridge overlooking the Jordan. I would like to make some sketches of it for this next academic year's assignment. Could we scape up enough to go there do you think?'

I liked the sound of this and we decided we could scrape up the necessary dough.

'There's still just enough time before term begins.'

'I've a large picture book of Belvoir Castle. In Hebrew it's called "Kochav ha Yarden", which is "Star of the Jordan".'

On this sudden impulse, we spent the next two hours booking the holiday.

Lastly we went through the first ten letters of the Hebrew alphabet, aleph to yodh and two of the vowel pointings.

Her thin pale forearms moved back and forth as she wrote the letters. She used more graceful or flowing movements than most of us do when writing.

I would buy some broad-tipped calligraphy pens and practice drawing the twenty-two consonants.

I set off for the Annex a little before midnight.

The main road bends before the Tickell Lane turn-off, but some way before that I could see flashing blue lights reflected in various windows.

A crowd of perhaps twenty people had gathered, whilst an ambulance and two police cars with their flashing lights and an off-road four-by-four belonging to the regional electricity company were bumped up on pavements.

Emma and Duncan, arm in arm, told me parts of the story.

One of the cast-iron Victorian gas lamps, which had been converted to electricity, had a loose access cover, known it seemed to some mischievous kids. As a prank they had removed it and connected its live terminal with a length of wire to the passenger door handle of a large limousine.

There was a suspicion that they had occasionally done this before as a lark and given other car owners shocks.

A fairly heavy-weight middle-aged fellow – lying flat on his back in the middle of Tickell Lane – had just been pronounced dead by the ambulance crew.

The shock had stunned his heart and stopped it, it seemed and although a couple of good thumps on the chest will often restart such a paralysed heart, the time lag before anyone thought of this had been too great.

Then a third police car drew up and a superintendent climbed out.

Then I spotted the supercilious, tall white male as he approached the superintendent.

I slipped away inconspicuously.

*   *   *   *

We flew out on Monday the twenty-eighth of September from Heathrow with El Al, the Israeli national airline. The gate was 'Gate J', very much set apart from the other gates and heavily guarded by airport police armed with sub-machine-guns.

We hired an older Land Rover Defender, which given some of the rough tracks we were to encounter, was probably a good choice.

We stayed in a small hotel in Tiberias, on the western shore of the Sea of Galilee, run by Pascal and Véronique Bouvier.

After a night's sleep, we ate breakfast on a terrace edged with pale pink-white tamarisks and gazed out over the pale-blue and chrome ripples on the shimmering lake, with a tall copper coffee-pot and rolls and various conserves in front of us. I entertained myself trapping wasps in a small dish of honey.

We drove southward and up to the ruins of Belvoir Castle high above the Jordan Valley, where after a wander round its walls and roofless chambers, we settled down under a large shady terebinth.

It had been built mostly with large, square-hewn basalt blocks – very hard, porous and of a dull sooty black colour – which had been quarried so as to create the surrounding ditch, but its arches, corbels and the more finely chamfered stones were of a white and more easily worked limestone. The blocks were cut very accurately and fitted exactly together with no mortar. The dark grey with the soft white touches was – despite its practical origin – quite pleasing.

Imogen sat in a straw sun-hat and a long-sleeved henna-coloured-coloured frock with a large sketch pad and drew me as I sat in the partial shade of a date-palm against a back-drop of the heat-distorted sun-soaked and remote hills on the eastern side of the Jordan.

I tried to imagine the crusading knights in their shiny armour and their sleeveless surcoats with their bright heraldic emblems, of their living habits and their everyday chores whilst stationed here.

Megan messaged me from Harlech to ask if this holiday meant that another break-in was imminent?

At lunch-time we bought falafels and hummus with plastic beakers of pomegranate juice from a mobile food van in the car park.

There were very few tourists at Belvoir, perhaps because it is one of the less spectacular of the Crusader castles.

The next day we paddled in the pale milky green waters of the Jordan, under the overhanging willow-like trees. We sat on some large stones on the bank and watched as shoals of tiny dark fish nibbled at any exfoliating skin on our feet; a free pedicure.

On day three, Imogen having managed to buy an old rickety easel, we returned to Belvoir. Her box of just six or seven paints were enough it seemed for rough drafts.

In a low vault some shallow graffiti had been etched into the stones. The only word I could perhaps decipher was 'd'este' which could be Old French or Provençal for 'of summer'.

Imogen sketched a peasant girl with her cuffs turned back, picking black-currants on a dusty hillside under a hot sun. How can anyone capture these things so effortlessly?

In the evening after dinner – chicken Alexander and a Cypriot *rosé* called Bellapais – we sat on the terrace, sipped coffee and ate sugar-dusted figs. Sometimes we read, sometimes Pascal would chat to us. 'We're from Toulouse, but seven years ago decided to leave. Véronique's father's Jewish and so we chose here ... where a bit of sanity still prevails.'

We listened.

'I feel sorry for the people of France, but the politicians ... and many others ... have just put their heads in the sand.'

'In Shakespeare, a Roman general called *Coriolanus*, cuts off the corn supply to some rebellious rabble.'

The wash-basin in our room was a brass bowl, beaten with the small regular dents of a round-headed hammer. It had perhaps come from a Jewish kitchen where Talmudic laws for the cleansing of cooking utensils demand a number of such, each with a discrete purpose.

On day four, we drove south to Beit She'an, from where we took the recently re-opened Jezreel Valley Railway to Haifa. The valley was broad and flat-bottomed, fertile, full of grain fields and other crops. There were rolling hills in the distance, very few trees and the air was dry. The trains and stations were all modern and clean.

I told Imogen a little of Eirig.

'He lacks confidence, but perhaps that will come with devotion and love.'

She nodded. 'He sounds good. The flip side is men who are too *macho* ... and usually just ridiculous.'

'A lot of men have difficulty in adjusting to today's world.'

Imogen gave a laconic tilt of the head.

In Haifa we changed onto a train to Acre and walked along the dusty boulevards into that ancient port city which figures in our school history books during the closing battles of the Crusades.

In the old bazaar, we sought a present for Matthew. A jeweller's shop sold old coins. A dinar minted by the Almoravid Berbers in Morocco in the twelfth century had been struck with trans-Saharan gold from Mali, it said. We examined it.

'North Africa's not his line.'

'We can't read Arabic and anyway, it'll cost a bob or two ... more than we have ... '

'It might be a forgery too? The wear looks suspiciously even and the strike's perfectly centred.'

Then we found a reproduction of the Monet painting *Le train dans la neige*, something much more up Matthew's street.

We strolled along the eastern stretch of the Land Wall with ice-creams, but did not visit the citadel or the excavated headquarters of the Hospitaller Knights. Belvoir was perhaps enough of a fix for us of medieval stonework.

At Haifa between changing trains, we paddled in the Mediterranean and watched some little chicks wading at the water's edge, I suppose just to say that we had done it.

Medieval life was based on faith. Liberty had as yet no meaning. And men did not *think*, they *knew*.

We read of the return to Jerusalem of Jews under Nehemiah, authorised by King Artaxerxes I. 'So we repaired the wall. We joined all its parts together and rebuilt it as far as half its height. Then the Arabs, the Ammonites and the Ashdodites plotted to come and destroy us, so we kept our swords close by us.'

On day five we strolled round Beit She'an, the Beth-shan of the Bible, where King Saul's body had been nailed to a wall.

Under a parasol at a ramshackle café, we devoured Black Forest *gâteau* and *café au lait* whilst writing postcards to my family, to Matthew, to Imogen's father and to Eirig.

Caravans had once come here from across the desert, trading aloes, spices, ebony and perfumes for silks and salt, gold and gum.

Our last day was spent in antique shops.

Large rusty nails were for sale, allegedly from a sunken Phoenician merchant vessel, which divers had nicknamed *Baal Hammon*, a Punic deity.

Megan would have called it a 'pubic deity'.

We looked at a Tyrian shekel, the only coin accepted in New Testament times for paying the Temple tax. You had to first buy a shekel – or a half shekel – with your Roman denarii. The Temple tax had been a half-shekel per year per adult male.

Imogen bought a cheap, unidentified and very worn coin, the size of a modern penny but wafer thin. It had square letters and a squashed face in the middle. Probably it had been minted by the crusaders. 'Something to try to puzzle out on a winter's evening,' she said.

When we arrived back in Oxford, Imogen smiled and gave me a kiss on the cheek as we parted. 'Perhaps that's enough travel for this summer?'

CHAPTER THIRTEEN

I answered the Annex's front door to Mervyn Grieff.

'Miss Hughes?'

I smiled. 'Yes. Miss Z. Q. Hughes.'

He smiled too. 'That's the one.'

He wore pin-striped trousers, a bow-tie and a dark grey jacket, but it lacked its court-room pink carnation in its button-hole.

'May we talk?' His shiny cheeks bulged hamster-like as if packed with handkerchiefs.

I led the way to the upstairs kitchen. 'There's only me in the building.'

'Good.' He sat down. 'The girl whom Carole had earmarked for Clytemnestra's Ghost has ulcerative colitis which has suddenly flared up ... and that's genuine.'

'Well, that makes it less awkward?'

'She's lost a lot of weight apparently and looks quite poorly.'

'I'm sorry about that,' I said with sincerity.

He produced a miniature bottle of Armagnac brandy. 'Shall we share this?'

'No, I'll have tea, but carry on.' I found a clean tumbler for him. The tip of his nose was pink.

'I understand that you know something about a robbery of precious metals in Ireland ... in 2012?'

'Yes. My father was in the Army. He mentioned it.'

'Do you know where these pieces of silver, gold and platinum now are?'

'Er ... some of them.'

'The gold bars are valued at close to a million pounds each.'

'Oh?'

'However two of the five are no longer with their siblings.'

'Abducted?'

'Yes ... lost and gone forever.'

'Like Clementine in the 1849 Californian gold rush song?'

'The first fence escaped with them ... but lost all the others.'

'To a second fence?'

'Gold is purified by melting it and stirring it, then as the impurities rise to the surface they are skimmed off.'

'That's described in the Old Testament.'

'So the origin-defining proportions of the impurities – of which silver, copper, zinc and iron are the commonest – are lost.'

I imagined Solomon's metal workers at Ezion Geber stirring a shallow crucible above a huge fire. A blast furnace for copper had also been found there at the head of the Gulf of Aqaba.

Mervyn spoke softly. 'Sophie, I suggest we become partners? Fifty-fifty?'

'I don't want any stolen money.'

He gave me a slightly barbed, though not unfriendly smile, a diplomat seeking a way round some minor impasse. 'Students run up large debts these days?'

'I'm not a student.'

He took a swig of his Armagnac. 'Do you have private means then?'

'No.'

'Think for a moment ... this could be life-changing?'

'It could. In more ways than one.'

He exhaled.

'Mervyn, you're a top lawyer. You represented a corrupt police superintendent who was in league with a London fence? Why?'

'It's not unlawful to defend a criminal.'

'Do you know how he knew about the hand-over in Northumberland?'

'No.'

'His former floosie works in M.I.6.'

He gave me a long uneasy look, then downed the rest of his brandy.

Having little physical appeal, he had probably been pleased to tie the knot with any woman and money – or the Midas touch even – he still believed, was the key to freedom.

'I intend to tell The Ulster Bank where the remaining stolen bars are and to claim the reward. I suggest you keep clear of this whole business.'

He thought hard. 'So M.I.6 have someone inside Sinn Féin?'

'My Great-Aunt Ceinwen lived hand-to-mouth. She never travelled farther than Aberystwyth or Shrewsbury, yet was blithe and kind ... and wholly disinterested in politics or wealth. She was one of the last infant teachers to have been asked to stay on as a teacher when her own schooling ended ... and she retired when she was seventy-six.'

He half-acknowledged the impressiveness of this. 'Not a modern-day heroine though ... because the world has changed.'

'It's said she was so good with the little ones.'

'Well ... perhaps I am being selfish ... but today life is tough. With only a little money, you have to accept poor treatment. If you're well off, you can stand your ground ... adopt a more "take it or leave it" stance?'

I sipped my tea. 'Mervyn, forget this whole affair ... or you'll end up in trouble. I am giving you good advice.'

'Oh.'

Have you heard of "Operation Plum Pudding"?'

That line came out of my mouth, but not out of my mind. I do not know where it came from.

He stared at me, thanked me reluctantly and I showed him out.

It is always childishly gratifying to be five or six inches taller than your opponent. I watched from my first-floor window, as outside he folded his body into his bright orange Lotus Evora and drove off.

'So "called to the bar" ... but which type of bar; gold, prison or chocolate?'

I wrestled with Biblical Hebrew for a bit. The first four letters – aleph, beth, gimel and daleth – are almost the A B C D of our own Roman alphabet. The third Greek letter is gamma. In Latin too, the early 'g' often becomes a 'c'. Gaius for instance, changes to Caius.

In Roman wedding ceremonies, the groom is referred to as 'Gaius' and the bride by its feminine form 'Gaia'. The bride at one point says, *'Ubi tu Gaius, ego Gaia,'* which means, 'Wherein you are the groom, I am the bride.'

I thought of Eirig. The Latin for ring was *gyrus*.

Unexpectedly Dusty rang the door-bell.

I gave her a bright smile. 'Come in.'

'Sorry Sophie, but I needed to leave the house. Mum and Digby are having another ding-dong. I can barely stand it.'

I sucked through my teeth. 'A bowl of soup?'

In my room, I showed her my first baby steps with Biblical Hebrew.

I had written out; 'He gave gold to the king and he gave oil to the prophet.'

She peered at the unfamiliar letters. 'I saw Stegosaurus in town yesterday ... in a Social Justice Activists' march.'

'Oh.'

'They wish to outlaw all Christian beliefs.'

'On which our civilisation is grounded.'

'His name's Steg Abajian. His father's Armenian, although he actually comes from Manchester.'

'Given his lisp, it's lucky it's not "Spencer". The irony of those with a lisp is that they cannot say "lisp".'

'He said to us that anyone who insulted a Moslem's beliefs, should be burnt alive ... or in some way be killed.'

I stirred the soup. 'In Britain, for some centuries, we've been governed in a mostly honest and competent way.'

'At my primary school, literacy, numeracy and discipline were being more and more eroded by nonsense "guidance" subjects ... so much time was wasted.'

'One more year and you'll be at university ... then good times will happen.'

She grinned. 'I've decided to apply for Japanese.'

'Good.'

'My grandad brought some Japanese bullets home from Burma. He'd emptied the powder out of them. He had had an officer's sword too, but the kit-bag it was in went astray on the troopship home.'

The soup was cock-a-leekie. I found some buns and butter.

'Japanese etiquette is very strict, however as a sort of counter-weight you can indulge in fantasies. You could go out into the shops in Kobe say, in a Jane Austen empire-line dress or some Peter Rabbit outfit and no one would poke fun at you or think you mad.'

'That's quite strange?'

'Is experimentation good for us?'

'I don't know.'

'On a reverse scale, I often meet people and think, "Why are you so envious or so full of scorn?" A little bit of fantasy might loosen up their rigidity.'

'Less motivated people might benefit from that ... as would certainly the fanatics. If you suggest adopting our ways, they reply, "This is not *your* country. The whole world belongs to Allah. It is you who must change."'

'Let's talk about something else.'

'Yes. I'm reading a book titled, *The Origins of the Latin Language*. It was first spoken in the plain of Latium, south of the Tiber – as its name suggests – and although changes were always occurring, it was quite stable from around eighty B.C. to fourteen A.D., the period of Classical Latin.'

I listened to her for a time, then – as we said good-night – whispered, 'Hopefully things will have cooled down by the time you're home.'

I drove the long road up to Cairnryan on Loch Ryan in south-western Scotland, caught the early evening ferry over to Larne and spent the night at a bed and breakfast in Carrickfergus.

It had rained and been windy on the crossing, but the light green seascape, the salt spray, the gulls and the grey cliffs seen through the mist, reminded me again of how I would like to be free from big-city life.

Next morning I entered the Corinthian-columned frontage of The Ulster Bank in Belfast's Donegall Square.

The receptionist had such a thick northern Irish accent – the classic 'head in a bucket of water' effect – that he had to go and fetch another staff member.

'Don't worry,' she said, 'we can't understand him either.'

I asked if I could speak to someone in security. When I explained that I knew the whereabouts of some gold bars, stolen in 2012, she looked at me askance, as if trying to judge my mental state.

Eventually I was ushered into an upstairs office with an older gentleman who evidently had heard of this robbery back in 2012.

He asked for some identity, which I gave him and which he studied carefully.

I had retrieved my one remaining dense one-kilogram platinum bar from under the shed and this I now placed on his blotter.

His eyes widened a little. He telephoned a secretary and asked her to bring a file.

As with the far less valuable silver one, my two platinum ones had been assayed, hallmarked, numbered and had – this time – 999.5 stamped on them to give their degree of purity.

'I know where most of the bars are hidden.'

'Not all?'

'I think some are missing.'

His secretary appeared with the file and he asked her to bring two cups of coffee and some biscuits.

He checked the number of the bar before him against a list of numbers.

'You are aware that this is stolen property?'

'I did not steal it. I merely found it ... and am returning it to its owner.'

He exhaled slowly. 'It is thought that two of the gold bars were taken to London, where they have almost certainly been melted down.'

'Oh.'

'Do you have any more in your possession?'

'No, but I believe there's a reward for the recovery of the remainder?'

'Er ... there was, but it may have lapsed ... or been withdrawn?'

'Well, could you un-lapse it?'

He managed a hint of a smile. 'Sophie, the police will want to know the location?'

'Perhaps, but I'm not obliged to tell them.' I felt particularly phlegmatic.

Over coffee, he asked a little about my current job and spoke of a few topical financial matters. A hint of friendliness emerged as he gauged that I was being straight.

I asked for a receipt for the platinum bar and this he wrote out on headed note-paper and signed. Someone would contact me soon, having looked into the question of rewards.

In the ship's lounge on the return trip, I read a twelve-page booklet, *The Rules of Netball*.

No one knew why I had been to Belfast. I had made up a story about an old N. & N.S.R. carriage body found on a farm being used as a hen coop.

On Sunday, the day before term officially began, eight of us met up on an outdoor netball court.

A distant sun and a cool breeze together were quite 'bracing'.

Helena was tall and agile, Katia the Greek girl never dropped the ball, Mie-Mie, the Burmese girl always did – and she never called her homeland 'Myanmar', but always 'Burma' – whilst Imogen, though quite lithe, lacked much in the way of eye-to-hand co-ordination.

'Could we meet up tomorrow evening for a second practice?' asked Helena.

No one seemed eager.

'It would be *nice* if come Christmas, we're not at the bottom of the league?'

'Have you checked to see if there's a booby prize?' asked Heather.

Helena did not find this amusing.

*　　*　　*　　*

Anyone registered with the University can attend its lectures; even if they are not on that particular course.

At the first of Simon Cumming's talks in the new term, I sat incognito at the back in an old tiered lecture theatre with hard oak benches. Emma came and sat beside me. 'Curious?'

'Yes.'

A gangly youth on the row in front turned round. 'Did I see you with Dr Sleight in Waterstone's coffee-shop?'

'Possibly.'

'How is it that you call him "Matthew"?'

I shrugged. 'He told me to.'

'When I tried, he growled, "It's 'Dr Sleight' or 'Sir' to you, Tompsett."'

Simon arrived, his Bermuda shorts revealing his knobbly knees. He dumped some books on the table at the front, then gazed out of a side window for a minute.

'Today's lecture is entitled "Cakes for the Baalim",' he informed a passing cloud before turning to face us.

'To beautify their temples, the Phoenicians used in particular cedar wood because of its enduring aromatic perfume. Up from the Red Sea came gold, peacocks and other precious woods to adorn their sanctuaries. To please their gods, the Canaanites offered gifts; statues, jewellery, coins and jars of perfume have all been found buried in their temple ruins. They believed that wealth and good fortune came from the gods.

King Hiram of Tyre and Solomon in Jerusalem were true friends it seems. Hiram sent cedar and masons to help build the temple to Yahweh in Jerusalem and in return received villages and abundant gold.'

Simon spoke of a recipe, of a cake offered in these Canaanite temples.

'Half an ephah of flour, water, a little milk, salt and leaven … and perhaps to especially honour the god, some raisins?'

He crossed the floor.

'The word "baalim" is the plural of "baal", meaning lord.' He wrote the word 'Baalah' on the board. 'The feminine ending "ah" makes it a female baal and "-at" is the feminine plural.

Now Sidon had a port, narrow streets and a market. It exported dried fruits, wines, wheat, cotton, glass-ware, silver, copper, salt, but above all cedar wood for building ships, temples and palaces … and its resin for embalming mummies.'

I could almost imagine myself amid the hectic hubbub of this Levantine town, set three millennia back in time, perhaps as a merchant invoicing the goods being laded onto a ship at the quayside?

A slide showed an ancient papyrus.

'Pharaoh, for a ship load of cedarwood paid five jars of gold and ten sacks of lentils … although that seems an odd mix. Either the word "thousand" is implied or they were exceptionally good lentils.'

Flights of stone stairs, courtyards, armaments, poems in Egyptian and Babylonian … so much had been uncovered there.

Simon jumped about a lot. 'Don't take notes. Don't work at spinal reflex level … just soak it up.'

We were doing.

'True prophets are not magicians or conjurors. Their ways are simple, unaffected … cutting up vegetables.'

I whispered to Emma, 'O'Rourke, is he still after Matthew's blood?'

'I expect so ... there's always some unburnt gunpowder in his psyche.'

I nodded.

'That guy who was electrocuted, a police inspector with two sergeants appeared. They wanted to know if anyone had taken pictures and if so, we were to delete them. Such instructions are bound to raise curiosity and so be counter-productive.' She showed me a shot of a bloated white face. 'So what was so special about this guy?'

I shrugged and shook my head.

*   *   *   *

Madame Dominique Wallis lived at Eynsham in a bijou town-house.

Her manner was Chopinesque. She wore a Japanese silk chemise and smoked using an amber cigarette holder which she wafted around. She exuded that kind of superiority indispensable to true 'artistes'.

We sat down on a blue-and-gold-upholstered *chaise longue*.

'The Ghost of Clytemnestra is not a broken woman. She's on the war-path, determined to see her killer punished.'

We studied my speech and decided which lines required a bitter invective and which a softer touch as I confided my thoughts to the audience.

Avoidance of melodrama would make it more Shakespeare, less Racine, more subtle ... less circumlocutory.

Shakespeare had luckily not heard of Aristotle's rules about plays; that the action should fall within a twenty-four hour span, have a fixed number of sub-plots, a fixed arrangement of lead parts and such like; the very strait-jackets which made eighteenth-century European drama so stilted.

My movements, under the pale-blue spot-light had to be exactly planned. The dazed half-slumbering Furies would groan only drowsily in response to my prods and insults.

My part felt to be acquiring 'shape', that word so beloved of musicians; 'Give it shape,' they are always saying, which I suppose refers to the dynamics, variations in tempo and such.

Wednesday afternoons were kept free of lectures for sports activities.

We lost our first netball fixture six to sixteen, but given that sixteen is itself a low score, it was not a total rout.

'We were quite good in defence,' I said encouragingly.

'Or,' replied Helena, 'Saint Anne's Belles are almost as bad as we are.'

'Anyway,' Heather put in, 'let's just enjoy it.'

I walked with Heather back into town and as we passed the Botanic Gardens, we saw a traffic warden inspecting an illegally parked car. The first three numbers of its registration plate were 251 followed by an isolated D and then another three numbers. I knew this to be a 'CD' or 'Corps diplomatique' plate.

'That belongs to the Master's boyfriend,' said Heather.

'The Russian?' I queried.

'The numbers 251 define it as Russian apparently.'

The traffic warden started writing a note, though presumably not a fine, when its driver reappeared and gave him two fingers.

'I wonder what he has in that rucksack,' asked Heather.

I pretended to listen. 'What's that? Tick-tock, tick-tock?'

The Russian pressed the accelerator so hard, such that his car's rear wheels spun and threw out lots of gravel, as if trying to kill the traffic warden with grape-shot.

Next day, Imogen had to attend a course-work 'sitting' in the art department. You had four hours in which to sketch and paint the 'sitter'.

I was curious to see this art department and Imogen had asked if I could come and sit at the back.

The invigilator was to be Dr Mpofu and he agreed. 'So long as she fetches us cups of coffee half-way through.'

We arrived at eight-fifteen in a room the size of a small gymnasium, where Imogen sat down at one of the semi-circle of fourteen easels and set out her brushes and paints.

Her clothes were as usual plain; a black skirt, a white T-shirt and a paint smock with ties down the back.

The sitter appeared and was positioned – her upper-half naked – with a red and green flag draped around her shoulders.

Mpofu said that the students could begin and had until a half past twelve. 'You do not have to recreate exactly the image which is falling onto your retinae. You may adjust the focus, the background and the ambience. The result though must still be a female figure – recognisable as Poppy ... and in this posture.'

She vaguely reminded me of the famous Delacroix picture in the Louvre, of the bare-breasted 'Liberty' or 'Marianne', waving her *tricolore*.

I sat at the back with a book.

To Imogen's left, an Hispanic-looking student – with a comically furrowed brow – painted with incredible intensity. The result though was just an unattractive muddle.

He, I learned later was Emiliano, the son of a deposed South American dictator. He had received a 'special scholarship' since his father had – coincidentally of course – donated half a million dollars to his college's funds.

Imogen transformed Poppy into Kundry, the 'Rose of Hell', from Wagner's *Parsifal*, cursed to live forever because she laughed at Christ's pain on the cross. This sorceress and the evil magician Klingsor were thwarted in their wickedness by the faithfulness of the knights. Poppy's face was depicted as mauve and contorted and her skirts and headband were in vivid reds and blues. The whole was a bit slap-dash, yet it sent a shudder down your spine.

I took an occasional discreet photo to record its progress.

Morag, on Imogen's right, showed a slightly similar train of thought

Melisende, Queen of Jerusalem, sat on a crude wooden medieval throne in an unnamed Crusader castle, with a slightly bent gold crown and draped round her shoulders and over her breasts the flag of Jerusalem. This is unique in heraldry for usually metal on metal is not permitted, but this – the exception – consists of gold on silver.

Its primitive medieval style had also in common with Imogen's picture, a sort of sophisticated naïvety.

I doodled on my note-book this flag of Jerusalem, which is a white background with five yellow crosses on it. A large yellow cross potent is in the middle, then in each of its four quadrants, four small plain Greek yellow crosses.

One student had Poppy holding a bomb, the stock

black ball with 'bomb' chalked crudely on it in white and a lit fuse fizzling away. Her other figures had turned their backs to Poppy and were hiding their eyes.

Just before eleven, I nipped down the back-stairs to a little coffee stall and returned with sixteen coffees in cardboard cups and a bag full of little tubs of milk and packets of sugar. Luke declared a ten-minute break.

Another picture I glimpsed, showed Poppy as a courtesan holding a closed fan and sitting on a balcony in Venice. It was a bit Picasso-like, made up of coloured squares, oblongs and circles and quite two-dimensional. The idea was good but the girl did not come alive, did not have character.

Half an hour before the end, a student – to judge by his appearance – came up the back-stairs and looked around.

I pretended not to notice. Imogen's coat lay on a table with other bags and jackets. It was a well-scuffed old brown leather coat which had been her mother's. It was knee-length, of cow-hide and perhaps had a sentimental attachment since her mother had worn it in her own youth.

He took it and tried to leave discreetly, but I was after him. In the corridor I grabbed him, shouted and started a general hullabaloo.

He broke free and fled.

I returned with the coat and everyone rotated back to their two-foot canvas squares.

CHAPTER FOURTEEN

Imogen and I met up again on the Saturday.

We bought six bottles of a wine called 'Cummings Valley' from New Zealand and a chocolate cake and went to call on Simon who also lived in Observatory Street.

'October the seventeenth is his birthday and as far as I know he has no family close by. He gives eight lectures a week, which is quite a load, especially given that some lecturers give hardly any.'

'He was once a clergyman though is now simply a sheep ... and a very black one. The story of his defrocking is quite colourful ... that's if black counts as a colour?'

It was six in the evening, the sky overcast. A light was on in Simon's front room but the patterned curtains were closed. There was no noise to suggest a party or other visitors.

We knocked.

After quite a wait the door opened gingerly.

Simon stood there in the nude except for a T-shirt which was rolled up and held with safety-pins at nipple level. Round his genitals he was clutching a white bath-towel which was quite evidently blood-stained.

He stared at us. 'Next door ... fetch Mr Brownlee. He's a retired surgeon.'

I dashed to the door indicated and hammered on it. A lean, kindly looking, septuagenarian answered. It was the man who had asked after Judith some ten weeks before.

'Mr Brownlee? Come quickly please ... your neighbour's bleeding quite badly.'

He came and we went through to the kitchen at the back of Simon's house.

Clearly he had sat on a stool and managed to cut off his testicles, which together with lots of bloodied swabs and bits of suture were in a bucket.

Mr Brownlee rolled up his shirt sleeves and knelt down on a cushion so as not to bloody the knees of his trousers, since the linoleum floor had plenty of blood on it.

Simon had acquired a scalpel, various forceps and stainless steel dishes which he had sterilised by putting them in the oven at a high temperature.

The key element apparently is to clamp the spermatic cords before you cut off the testicles, then not merely ligature them but transfix them. This it seems means that you push the needle through the cord a couple of times so that the ligature cannot slip off.

Luckily the spermatic cords had not retracted and Mr Brownlee was able to get hold of them. He then flooded everything with surgical spirit, watched for a time to see that no small bleeders needed tying and then quite crudely stitched the scrotal incision back together.

Imogen and I spent our time putting bloodied items into a thick plastic bin-bag, cleaning areas of the floor and washing this or that.

Mr Brownlee then watched Simon's scrotum for some time to be sure that no haematoma was developing.

Simon had bought lots of sterile swabs and surgical sutures, but when he could not control the bleeding he had just squeezed everything with the bath-towel and so lost the sterility which he had at first tried hard to maintain.

Mr Brownlee sat down on a chair and Imogen made four mugs of tea.

'Simon, why did you do this?'

'Well ... partly because I suspect that false sex claims might be made against me ... but also because I am sure in my own mind that I am not going to marry. I am happy with my own company and my books.'

Mr Brownlee thanked Imogen for the tea. 'We must keep this between ourselves if possible ... ' Here he glanced at Imogen and myself and we both nodded strongly in the affirmative. 'If it becomes infected and you have to go into hospital, well then ... it may well come out, but if it does you will probably be struck off the teaching register.'

There being no sign of swelling, he gave Simon a last thorough dowsing with surgical spirit and applied a self-adhesive dressing to the wound.   '

'You're not depressed, you're not suicidal, you're not a danger to anyone, so in a way that would be unfair ... but I suspect that's just the way things are. All black and white, easy answers ... no one's interested in any finer reasoning.'

Simon who had hardly spoken a word, thanked the wise old surgeon in a husky, barely audible voice.

Mr Brownlee smiled, said he would be in all evening if needed and took his leave.

Simon went to bed, since the operation had left him weak and exhausted. Imogen and I spent an hour scrubbing and cleaning before we too left, also saying that he could ring us if he needed to.

We sat with him for a time before leaving and made him more tea to replace the blood loss.

'Someone told me that Opoku is cooking up another

sex scandal for me ... I thought this would be a good way to prove them wrong.'

'Why not just go to some quiet little market town and find a job stocking shelves in the local supermarket?' suggested Imogen.

'I might one day ... but I would miss teaching.'

In *The Bear* I said to Imogen, 'Well that was a birthday party to remember.'

We sat down in a quiet area near the window with our cheese rolls, crisps and grapefruit juices.

'Have the 'sitting' paintings been marked yet?'

'Yes. The Prof marked them. Morag and I came joint first. Marking paintings is a bit unique. You line them all up, then shuffle them around until you have the best at one end and the worst at the other.'

'You couldn't do that with essays.'

Imogen said, 'If Simon were homosexual, there would be no difficulty; that's on the white list. Cutting off your testicles though, puts you on the black list, but why? You can still lecture?'

'Those who cut off their testicles do not have strong political pressure groups behind them.'

'So the quangos in London can do what they want with them? What is the moral basis used by these highly paid "experts"?'

'I doubt there is one. It'll be about social modelling.'

'I so hope his wound doesn't become infected.'

'When Simon was a cathedral canon, he was a prebendary, which he liked to say meant "pre-bent".'

Imogen replied, 'That would be funny if it were not so true.'

'I've been to one of his lectures. He'll be a real loss if he is sacked.'

'The tin-pot dictators won't care a toss about that.'

*   *   *   *

I had unearthed an article from the long-folded Northumberland Courant about a runaway wagon on the N. & N.S.R.

I heard Alison come in from a music rehearsal.

'Tea?' I called.

'Yes please.'

She had calmed down over my becoming Clytemnestra's Ghost.

'That barcarolle from *The Tales of Hoffmann*,' she paused for breath, 'So exquisite. *Belle nuit, ô nuit d'amour*; Beautiful night, o night of love.'

I cut a cherry tart in two.

'As we were setting up in Saint Columb's, a group came in saying they had booked the crypt. We said that was fine since we were in the nave, but they seemed reluctant to do whatever it was they had planned and after some rather contrived excuses, left.'

'Oh.'

'Martin – the first horn – wondered if they were a group rumoured to enact old religious rituals?'

'Oh? A bit odd ... though I don't suppose it's illegal?'

'Unless it's an excuse for an orgy?'

'Does that need an excuse?'

'Dressing up as temple harlots ... as Bacchus? Perhaps it's exciting ... like a masque?'

I looked at her. 'You've given this thought.'

I described Lucinda and indeed one woman seemed to fit.

'Bridget, the mezzo-soprano, thought she caught a whiff of frankincense. The finest,' she said, 'is an almost white variety – *samr* – from trees on the coast of southern Arabia.'

Eirig pitched up and we lay on my bed. 'Would you like to be caressed?' he murmured.

I tilted my eyebrows inwards. 'Er ... yes. I'm like those silly country girls, who admit it when they like something. When the Victorian magistrate asked the pregnant milkmaid why she let the swineherd do it, she replied, "Because I loiked it, Sir."'

As he kissed my breasts and tickled my tummy, I laughed. *Une belle nuit, ô nuit d'amour.*

'Small but good.'

Even Megan's modest paps were larger than mine.

'I've met a lot of men since I came to Oxford Eirig, but it's only you I want. You do trust me? When this is all over we're going to ... '

'Have a little farm with sheep?'

'I think so.'

'But we have neither the money nor any farming experience.'

'Don't worry.' I looked into his eyes. 'You know that hymn, *Nearer my God to Thee?* It was written by Sarah Flower, who married the railway engineer William Adams, the inventor of the fishplate.'

'Those Victorians, they had such belief in themselves.'

*   *   *   *

Basil Fleet, a lawyer who was the uncle of my old Newcastle University flat-mate Mary, came with me. We met in a room rented for two hours in the Gateshead Hilton, with three of the staff of The Ulster Bank and a police inspector.

An armoured security van stood in the car park.

A well-groomed man in his fifties, Mr Prior, the bank's negotiator, did happily not attempt to play poker.

He smiled not unpleasantly.

'Our Achilles' heel was that we were not only the intended recipients of these seventeen bars, but also the insurers. They are therefore legally ours on both counts.'

He offered nine per cent of the market price of whatever was retrieved. I did not haggle.

Papers were signed.

Over coffee and buns, I learnt that platinum – though much rarer than gold – is only a little more expensive and that cast blocks of platinum tend to be called 'bars' father than 'ingots'.

Platinum coins were minted in Russia under Tsar Nicholas I, to use up the platinum which was a by-product from the silver and lead mines in the Urals and which had been noted to be corrosion resistant.

I led this strange four-vehicle convoy northwards with Basil in my passenger seat.

'I have warned them that one person would need suitable clothing to protect himself against mud and brambles and thorns.'

'The most junior of the bank's trio said he has some old clothes with him.'

We all bumped along the rough narrow track, stopped, climbed over the low barbed wire and netting fence and gathered ourselves together in a huddle. I explained where the hidden bars were.

My friend Mr Toro, in the next field, peered crossly over the dividing fence, evidently displeased not to be taking part.

The three large gold blocks were quickly found though locating the nine smaller bars took time.

However the day ended happily and we all agreed that the task had been successfully completed.

Photographs were taken; a bit like Howard Carter and his assistants being depicted outside the entrance to Tutankhamun's tomb with some of its treasures laid out at their feet.

Five days later my bank account rose to a level previously undreamt of.

At home in Oxford, Alison showed me an article from a local newspaper; Carole Grieff versus Gavin O'Rourke.

In court Mervyn had come unstuck at one point. He had used a Latin phrase and then apologised by saying that lawyers liked to use Latin. The fellow on the stand then replied in fluent Latin, which floored Grieff and caused a ripple of laughter.

Some of Mervyn's cultured pearls – as opposed to any natural ones – which he threw onto the floor of the court, were trodden into the dirt by the defending swine.

None the less, the documentary evidence was overwhelming and he won, the judge awarding Carole thirty-six thousand pounds in damages.

The judge also asked Mervyn if he wished legal expenses to be added to this.

'Er, yes. Fifty thousand pounds, if it please Your Honour.'

'Hmm ... how long did you spend preparing this brief?'

'About three hours Your Honour.'

'Hmm ... I'll give you thirty.'

*   *   *   *

'In mid-February,' I said, 'an event for launching independently published books is being held at Foyles, that well-known bookshop in London's Charing Cross Road ... and I've managed to reserve the last of the fourteen available tables for seven hundred pounds.'

'Oh?' said Matthew uncertainly.

'There will be around two hundred invites sent to those in the publishing and literary worlds and we should have T-shirts and bookmarks and posters printed.'

He smiled indulgently. 'You're very enthusiastic, but for a railway book, do you think it will do much?'

'Well, maybe not ... but at least it's a launch ... at least we are giving it a send-off.'

He softened, thanked me and gave his approval to my efforts.

I left his flat at around seven in the evening. Dusk was falling and I glimpsed a silhouette coming toward me from the Banbury Road direction. It had a vaguely familiar gait.

Lucinda's hair had quite suddenly turned grey and her face looked drawn. That well-kept brightness of forty-something had vanished and she was suddenly on the way to becoming an old woman.

She stopped and we looked at one another.

She was shaking slightly.

'Are you all right?'

She looked at me with hooded eyes and after some time replied, 'No, not really.'

'Can I do anything?'

There was a long clumsy pause. 'Do you want a cup of tea?'

In her kitchen I managed to piece together her sorry tale.

Digby had been two-timing her with some nineteen-year-old Nigerian student. She had thrown him out, but straight away become besotted with one Mehmet Halit Arslan, a Turk in his twenties, who had physically mistreated her and demanded that she cook curries for him twice a day. In addition she had now discovered that he had stolen almost twenty thousand pounds out of one of her bank accounts.

Having espoused a lie for so long – about the innate goodness of all one's fellow human beings – it is hard to admit that you were wrong.

We sat on her long grey sofa.

'Stupidly – wanting revenge I suppose – I made a long superficial cut down my left forearm and said he had done it. Of course its shallowness, length, straightness and the fact that I am right-handed gave away immediately that I had done it myself.'

She asked me to make tea, toast some stale bread and take out the cheese, butter and jam. I was becoming an expert on other people's kitchens.

It is strange how these people who are so keen to tell you of their noble ideals or their wonderful philosophies never are themselves the real thing when it comes to the crunch.

I wondered how long it had taken her to see that these friendships were built on sand? I was so lucky to have my simple loyal Eirig ... someone from my own background and therefore someone whom I properly understood.

'A week ago Mehmet went into a rage because planning permission had been refused for a mosque somewhere. I replied that when Christians were murdered or their houses burnt down in Pakistan or Buddhist shrines were desecrated in the Middle East, he never uttered a word against his co-religionists.

Then he hit me violently and left in a storm.' She half-removed her blouse and showed me a large bruise on her upper left arm.

I took a deep breath. 'If Allah is telling them to conquer the whole world, that all non-Moslems are the enemy ... or at least only there to be scorned or used, then ... ? Did you go to the police?'

'Yes. They knew him. They said he had done the same thing before.'

Accidentally she spilt some milk, but it was easily mopped up.

'If we close our eyes to terrorism or wickedness ... or even deny it ... are we not then guilty of wrongdoing also?'

She spread some brie on her toast.

'How much does Dusty know?'

'Everything ... and she's been so good.' She broke down and wept.

After spreading butter and jam on my own toast, I mentioned Dusty's interest in applying to university to read Japanese. 'Don't stop her Lucinda ... let her do what she wants.'

'I have an older Swedish colleague, who says that in Sweden they used to think that in running our empire we were very harsh and unenlightened. He ended by saying, "But now we understand."'

I was nodding so much that I feared my head might roll off.

I replied, 'America has huge racial and crime problems, but at least they're open about it ... unlike here or in Scandinavia where the truth is dubbed "inflammatory".'

Lucinda at last looked up and gazed at me. Her tears had abated.

'In Saint Columb's, do you pretend to worship Baal?'

'How do you know about that?'

'A girl in the Annex is a musician ... They ran into you all last Monday.'

'It's only a silly game ... an experiment to see if these new-moon rituals have any mystical effect?'

'Would not one event give you an answer?'

'We tried the Egyptian sun god, Ra, too ... Gavin O'Rourke played the pharaoh. Next we tried smoking from a hubble-bubble ... a mix of hashish and tobacco. The ball glowed red each time one of us drew on our tube.'

'Who was the god this time?'

'Allah. We prayed to his angel Harut, the one who taught sorcery to the Babylonians.'

Lucinda found some cherry tarts whilst I made more tea.

'Have you thought of starting a new life ... perhaps away from Oxford?'

'Yes and no. I love this house, but I might take early retirement. I've had enough of teaching. I might be allowed to leave early on grounds of ill health?'

'Then what would you do?'

'I don't know. Teach backward children to read? Learn to paint?'

'Learn to paint?'

'Not like Imogen ... just painting by numbers ... then maybe try watercolours?'

'When Matthew's book's launched and I finish here, I want to try sheep farming.'

'Sheep farming? Do you know anything about it?'

'No, but isn't anticipation half the fun?'

'Well the fun won't last for long if you become stuck?'

'Perhaps it's just a fantasy ... so I'll end up as a librarian ... or perhaps teaching Welsh somewhere, but I might regret it if we don't seize the chance ... driving your quad round the field a few times then home for lunch?'

She managed a smile. 'Or having a tantrum during a dry summer when the neighbour's sheep have managed to find a way through your hedges or netting and are eating *your* grass?'

I laughed too.

'Incidentally, who's the "we"?'

'Oh, it's Eirig.'

'What happened to Ceinlys?'

'Oh she's just a doll. We're not taking her on our honeymoon though, because if our baggage went astray and we lost her, Eirig would be very upset.'

'You could pay for a seat for her. There's a top-notch 'cellist in Oriel who does not want his very valuable 'cello in the hold being bumped by heavy suitcases, so he pays for a seat for it.'

'Back to Saint Columb's. Is Poppy the "temple harlot" in these pagan rites?'

Lucinda looked at me. 'You're very knowledgeable?'

'It was actually just a guess.'

'Her nickname is "Elissa", the feminine form of "el", god, apparently.'

'Is she paid?'

'Oh yes. That's her reason for being there ... ostensibly. She says that she's compelled to because of the stingy student grants.'

I raised my eyebrows.

'She's mentioned you. She thinks you don't like her?'

'How perceptive.'

She took me upstairs to her bedroom, opened her wardrobe and took out a blue knee-length skirt. Round its lower hem it had pomegranate-like tassels in blue, red and purple cotton which alternated with small gold-like coins.

Lucinda nicked the hem with a pair of scissors and then started to tear it into pieces.

'What are you doing?'

'I've finished with this rubbish too.'

I nodded gently. 'Did you rent out the flat again?'

'I was going to let it to an old class-mate who's leaving her husband ... but the council said that an asylum seeker had priority.'

'Who would not pay the rent?'

'No, the council said they would guarantee that, but I don't want lots of strange people in the building ... so I said it needed some renovation work.'

'Hmm ... we're only a few steps away from full-on communism.'

CHAPTER FIFTEEN

The third rehearsal of *The Eumenides* required my presence.

Wearing a white T-shirt and a black pinafore dress with a small rucksack slung from one shoulder, I looked quite student-like.

Saint Catherine's College consists wholly of modern buildings and in its glass-fronted foyer – where grey armchairs with wooden legs, small round coffee-tables and a coffee-dispensing machine were scattered – I sat with Apollo whilst Carole spent much time with the Pythian Prophetess, trying to capture an aura of supernatural horror.

The wardrobe girl measured me for a mid-calf-length Doric tunic, dark blue with lilac box-patterned edging to the hem. It would also be expertly ripped and have a huge blood stain superimposed on it.

Hermes appeared with coffee and a bun. 'Ah, fellow Thespians, I have a *ham roll*.'

We managed a smile.

Afterwards five of us went for a drink in *The Turf Tavern* and under its low and ancient beams sat at an oval table in the bay window.

Despite a love of the stage, all saw that after finishing their degrees, it would be more realistic to take accountancy exams or such. The higher mountains of the film and stage world were near impossible to climb.

'Amateur dramatics is just as exciting,' I urged.

David, the fellow playing Apollo, was quite military

looking. 'I'll probably end up helping my dad with his tree surgeon business.'

We sipped our wine and nibbled the cheese cubes and mini-gherkins on sticks.

Louise, our prompt, gave her definition of a good actor. 'It's one who if he loses his place, can *ad lib* until the prompter finds hers.'

She was doing a placement with the architects who were designing the new block of student flats for Newlove. 'Its being paid for by someone from the Gulf.'

'Purely as an investment?' asked David.

She reflected. 'Er ... there's a clause in the small print about having a representative on all College appointment committees.'

Rochelle, the Prophetess, read Russian. After naming O'Rourke's boyfriend, she said, 'Dostoyevsky says that if you deceive someone, you not only debase yourself, but you also damage the entire world.'

Back in the Annex, Alison handed me a parcel of twelve miniature bottles of Cointreau. The label read, 'From Mervyn. With sincere thanks.'

Alison and I each had one in her room and listened to Wagner's *Rienzi* overture with its wonderful and deep main theme.

'The originality, the chord shifts,' she sighed.

We dimmed the lights and let the music flow over us.

I thought of Eirig, the cherry on my cake. He was the sweetest – in fact the only real sweet – I have ever had.

The next day he and I drove to Brockhampton Court, a manor house built around 1425, the era just before the modern world – with its merchant classes, banking and greater freedom of travel – began.

I lay in the thick grass beside the moat, on as it were a rough straw palliasse, whilst Eirig sat astride me and tickled my nose with a dandelion.

My tongue explored the inside of my left cheek.

He bent down and whispered, 'Will you marry me?'

I grew deeply serious. I had known this moment would one day come. I hugged him. 'Eirig, I have to give you a chance to either ask that again ... or not to.'

'Oh?'

'You must keep this secret.' I eyed him.

'I will.'

'I do not have all my feminine bits ... so I cannot have children.'

He fell on me and wept. 'Will you marry me?'

I managed to restrain my tears. 'Yes. We have Ceinlys ... and maybe soon some sheep.'

We kissed.

In a medieval chapel nearby, a spiral stairway led up to a tiny gallery. A dim red lamp flickered above a stone altar, faintly illuminating the rough irregular stonework.

A knight and his lady lay on top of a tomb – dusty but dignified – with faded but coloured apparel, shield and sword all carved as one in stone.

Over coffee, we read the sheep farming chapter on how much grass a field will yield. It depends on the depth and alkalinity of the soil, its gradient, altitude, latitude, grass species, sward, clover, north-south exposure ...

'This is too complicated.'

It touched on how to use your fields less intensively, as in older small-scale methods of farming.

Supposedly it gave a guide as to how many sheep you could keep per acre, both in summer and in winter.

I felt that much of this you would learn only by experience or just common-sense.

Grass is a low cost feed but also important for the health of the flock. Your pasture should not be over-grazed.

'It's lovely to delve into knowledge which stretches back for millennia,' I said.

*   *   *   *

Beside the River Avon a small farm was for sale.

'It's only thirty-one acres,' I said to Eirig, as the windscreen wipers swished back and forth.

We met the estate agent in a lay-by and huddled beneath three umbrellas. 'The farmhouse is of Cotswold stone and solid, but the interior needs updating.'

'And there are two fields?'

'The soil and the pasturage are good. The one slopes downhill. The other is flatter, but it borders the river, which floods from time to time.'

'Still, grass always recovers,' Eirig chipped in.

'The current tenants – Donald Sneddon and his wife – have given notice and the owner wants to sell. They're moving back to Kirkcudbright and their tenancy expires at the end of January. They breed Charolais bulls, but he says it's been an uneven ride.'

'Oh. A rodeo?'

We walked down the stony track to the yard which was between the house and a rather ramshackle wood and stone barn. Here Mr Sneddon was driving his tractor round in circles with a bull tied to the back of it, a rope through the brass ring in its nose. He explained that at the bull market in Perth it had refused to budge when led into the arena, so he was making sure it knew the drill ready for the next trip.

'Farming's unpredictable,' he explained. 'We know our outlay for a year, almost to the penny, but the income can be anywhere.'

'This land's more suited to sheep,' added his wife. 'It's too uneven for arable farming.'

The rough open-fronted barn, would give enough cover for a tractor and a few other vehicles and bits of farm equipment, but the nearby steel-framed barn – if to be suitable for sheep in winter or during bad weather – would need to be altered. It would need to be made open-fronted for good ventilation and with bars and feeding troughs added.

Mr Sneddon spoke of steroids. 'Some bull breeders use them to produce heavier, meatier beasts, but you have to make a decision ... either to go that way or not.'

*   *   *   *

On the Monday morning I awoke stuffed with cold, so I stayed in bed.

Feverish, I floated in and out of a state of delirium, walking through unknown woods.

I played with the jigsaw pieces of the Galway to Belfast armoured van raid.

Had the M.I.6 girl with the scarab woolly heard about the transfer to Scotland from their man in the Dublin embassy who in turn had an agent inside Sinn Féin? And had they not passed the tip-off on to the British Army Command in Lisburn?

The grey armoured security van left Galway on a rainy evening in November 2012. It stopped in Athlone at Deas's Chippy. Did someone watch it as it turned northwards onto the N55 towards Cavan?

A tractor had lurched out from behind a hedge to block the road. Men in black Balaclavas appeared waving rifles. They pushed a slab of old Semtex – a Czechoslovakian-made plastic explosive from the Soviet era – beneath the security van and the crew climbed out with their hands up.

The ambushers fired shots into the air. Why? To prove their manliness? One nearly died. The fence in Northumberland were due to pay them in U.S. one-hundred-dollar bills.

And who might have been in the night ferry's cafeteria, not entirely focused on his breakfast?

I could almost see a crime novel here; with a few adjustments and a disclaimer. The I.R.A count their dollars before handing the bars to fence A. Fence A is then ambushed by fence B. Had someone made a little extra by tipping them off? Two members of fence A managed to escape with two gold ingots.

The ruse of killing their third member – who had put up a fight – by a simulated old Chinese custom, reminded me of a story about a fox near Dolgellau which had laid a trail of chicken feathers on a path opposite to the one it then took.

Next the leader of fence B foils his pals and steals the fifteen captured bars. His fellow crooks then frame him for the 'Chinese' murder ... Hafid investigates. Evidence against the 'pals' mysteriously disappears ... Mervyn enters ...

In one way, none of this mattered. I had received the reward.

I ate some soup, then went back to bed and slept.

Only some of the rooms in the Annex had numbers on their doors and mine did not.

Whilst trying to decolonise my throat again at two in the morning, I heard a board creak on the landing outside my door.

In early Japanese castles, some floorboards were intentionally laid to creak, to expose the intruder or the spy, since the rightful servants and soldiery knew where not to tread.

I opened up and as I had half-suspected, Roderick stood there in the gloom. I ushered him inside and locked the door.

'The sloppy old mortise locks here could probably be picked with a hair-grip,' I whispered as I waved him to the chair by the desk in the low light of my bedside lamp..

'Sophie, I've decided to bail out.'

'Oh?'

'I've had enough of trapping ne'er-do-wells only to be overruled by a judge who simply disagrees with the law.'

I understood.

'I arranged an audience with a high-level Whitehall mandarin and explained that I would like to retire immediately on a full pension and with a six-figure lump sum. After a few bemused moments, he pointed out that at fifty-five that was an impossibility. I then laid out my photographs of vehicles taken on a certain day near Cumberford and added that others existed which would identify the young man, the young woman and the sturdier older man.'

I told my former boss of the fellow trampled by cows and the more senior official ectrocuted by his car. 'What one might call a pair of spectacles?'

Roderick raised his eyebrows.

'My cousin's five-year old has a game called "Don't Scream". We could send a set to the Head of M.I.6.'

'You think he should be good at it by now?'

'I daresay.'

'My proposed pension arrangements proved possible and truly said, I'm just pleased to be out of it. Susan and I have a cottage in Devon.'

I nodded slowly.

'We'll grow vegetables, keep bees and join a local preservation railway as volunteers.'

I went to make tea for us.

'In my final days of work – I deleted as far as possible all links or references to you and to myself from our databases and shredded a few dozen documents.'

I removed the coarse red hessian cloth draped over my small copper-banded oak chest and turned the numbered rings on its brass padlock. With my pen-torch I pulled three photos in an envelope out from under the upper layer of boards in its bottom. 'I had a feeling you would come.'

He peered at them. 'Thank you. We thought briefly of retiring to Greece ... but the whiff of mixed oil, steam and coal dust ... it won the day.'

I smiled.

'Now that Matthew's book's finished, what are your plans?'

I looked at him. 'Well ... I've just become engaged and I've made an offer for a little farm which has been accepted, but ... it's not likely to be much of a success ... so, I'll just take each day as it comes ... and pray that we're not slung into prison for our past misdoings.'

'I think we're safe.... but it is an unpredictable world.'

'We fought back quite well.'

He gave an expressionless smile.

I smiled more brightly and we parted.

*   *   *   *

Out of the blue came a written request from Professor O'Rourke for a meeting.

In the Master's spacious and modern office, in a comfortable armchair at one end, sat a Middle-Eastern gentleman wearing a black woollen robe with a red cord round its middle, a red keffiyeh and the heavy black ring which holds it in place and which is called I believe, an 'agal'.

He rose and we shook hands politely.

'Achmed, this is Sophie. Sophie, this is Mr Achmed Alamgir, personal assistant to His Excellency the Emir Hasan of the United Arab Emirates.'

The 'desk end' of the room was in semi-darkness and I was waved to another of the armchairs around the circular coffee-table at the 'discussion end'.

Gavin opened the drinks cabinet. 'The Emir is financing a new student accommodation block here at Newlove.'

'Oh?'

'His son is currently at Harrow, but His Excellency would like him to come on to Oxford.'

Mr Alamgir asked for a whisky on the rocks and I a tonic water.

'Sophie, when I first heard of your appointment, I had my suspicions that you were to be Matthew's scout ... or *aide-de-camp* ... and events have borne this out?'

'Principally I helped him research his book.'

'Do you know of our past frictions?'

'Yes, but he is not vindictive. He is willing to let bygones be bygones.'

'Good, I too would like a truce.'

'That is simply done. Leave Matthew, Imogen and myself alone – and ensure that others do – and there will be no more Carole-Grieff-like *exposés*.'

His face suddenly reddened and its muscles tautened. 'Carole Grieff ... She's a tit ... a Neo-Nazi!'

I leaned backwards. The words 'tit' and 'Neo-Nazi', coming from the master of an Oxford college? Would you not expect something more considered or well-articulated? 'Neo-Nazi' does not mean anything. It is simply an insult.

'Are you yourself from the Gulf, Mr Alamgir?'

He eyed me inscrutably. 'I come from Alexandria.'

'Oh. Egyptians do seem to be the more cultured sector of the Arab world.'

'Thank you.' He smiled urbanely. 'We have a long history.'

O'Rourke having repressed his fury, rejoined the conversation. 'His daughter, Bilqis, works in Tehran and last week the morality police stopped her and fined her heavily since she had a whole inch of wrist showing.'

'Hmm,' I mused. 'Oxford's not quite there yet ... but soon?'

There was a moment of silence.

Newlove College's motto was, 'Courage and diligence.' Libby's take on it was, 'If you can't make it, fake it.'

I drank some tonic water. 'Professor, Mr Alamgir, may I tell you a story?'

'Please. We need some entertainment,' urged Mr Alamgir with a touch of dry humour..

'A school-friend of mine went on a pilgrimage with her family to Lourdes. They queued on the long causeway which leads to the grotto where the peasant girl had her visions of the Virgin Mary, awaiting their turn for a couple of minutes in this cave where there is also a spring and you can dab yourself.

In front of them was a man carrying a small girl of three or four, who probably had some sort of deformity or illness. Now so devout and ardent were the prayers of this man – presumably the father – that he went the entire distance along this causeway on his knees.' I ended by saying, 'That really is love and that is what counts.' I had given myself a lump in my throat.

I shook Gavin's and Achmed's hands and left.

I told Alison that O'Rourke had called Carole a Neo-Nazi.

She replied, 'If you had given an opponent thought, you would have a more real insight to share.'

'Not being a student and so not being at risk of being denied my degree, I was able to be quite ruthless with him.'

Alison had once visited Istanbul. 'There's a verse from the Qur'an on the door of the Topkapi palace which reads, "The heart of wisdom is the fear of Allah."'

'The Christian parallel,' I replied, 'is "The fear of the Lord is the *beginning* of wisdom."'

CHAPTER SIXTEEN

On bonfire night, Newlove College held a buffet and a barn dance in its main refectory.

I bought a double ticket, 'Resident plus one' and as Eirig was working, asked Dusty to come.

In the quad a bonfire of discarded packing cases and pallets blazed away, crackling and throwing off sparks into the night sky. A few exotic Catherine wheels and Roman candles lit up the cool crisp evening air, whilst trays of sparkling wine were brought round.

A straw-stuffed Guy with an oddly Puritan-style hat and a large pectoral cross burned readily enough, his punishment for unsuccessfully plotting against Parliament and the King.

The Reverend Elaine-Marie Gooch clinked glasses with me before she realised who I was.

'Oh, Sophie? You're only here for the Michaelmas term, yes? Not Hilary?'

I gave a dour smile. 'Are you pleased ... or delighted even?'

She grinned glacially before waltzing off in search of more exalted company.

She wore a navy leather coat. Its tight belt together with the way its lower part tapered inwards towards her knees, emphasised perhaps her wasp-like shape. Her dark hair was tucked into its upturned collar.

Did men long to ravish her? Did they sense events in the middle of the night which would make them sweat and blush?

The ticket-clipper tried to stick Rainbow badges onto our jackets, but we resisted.

Inside, Dusty and I sipped mulled wine and nibbled hot chestnuts.

With her coat removed and the semi-high-heels of her black leather boots tapping the steps up onto the stage, Elaine-Marie went to the lectern, rapped a gavel and began her welcome speech. She spoke of a wonderful world full of rich diversity and of a bold and overdue resistance to the unpalatable ways of an outmoded past.

Echoing some leading clergy, she described the Lord's Prayer as 'problematic' and spoke of the need for all religions to 'come together'.

Dusty – keen on her Roman history – compared Numa – Ancient Rome's second king – to Gavin. 'The nymph Egeria's guidance to him – in contrast to this rubbish – will have been pithy, straight and staunchly loyal?'

A five-pointed star rested on Elaine-Marie's breasts; the pentangle, the symbol of witchcraft; not the six-pointed Star of David.

My ears caught the phrase; 'Youthleth white helephants.'

Trevor, a lad with a Royal Navy cadetship explained that an early warning aircraft high above an aircraft carrier with its wide surveillance area, made it far less vulnerable to attack than say a frigate.

'Rule Britannia!' sneered Poppy.

I thought to say, 'Since most of our exports and imports come and go by sea, it makes sense to have a navy,' but there was no point.

Poppy glared at me, as if debating whether to summon another mob to duff me up.

Again, when a teenager, I might have retorted that refashioning her nose could only improve it, but now I just keep mum.

I told Dusty of the farm. 'Churchill said that success is failure followed by failure but without a loss of enthusiasm.'

Around us we heard dribs and drabs of dialogue, mostly *passé*, pea-shooter stuff.

Someone was flying to Maryland for Christmas. One mindless couple left early, Cinderella-like; as if sex had to happen before midnight.

The Master with his boyfriend, almost collided with us. The hairs in his nostrils quivered slightly.

'Good evening, Professor.'

'Ah ... Alexei, this is Sophie.'

'Good evening.'

'No Rainbow badge? You're meant to wear one, to show that you *approve* of freedom.'

'And *you* should allow a choice, to show that you *really* approve of freedom.'

Gavin took Alexei's wrist and led him away.

Burke said that if you surrender your judgement to the opinions of others, you become a nonentity; like one enchanted and led by a Pied Piper.

Elaine-Marie sacrificed nothing in a bid for freedom. She shunned the hardship of truthfulness and paddled down a river devoid of rocks or rapids ... but perhaps with a big whirlpool at its end?

I said to Dusty, 'If you're lacking something ... salt for instance, then your taste-buds say, "I want a bacon buttie." Does not the mind work like that too?'

She thought. 'I suppose so ... but we often suppress it?'

I thought of my potential sheep. Morning prayer or the Army's 'Part One orders' are at least a guide for the day.

Dusty whispered., 'Nothing here to buckle our diaphragms.'

We left, bumping as we did so, into a red-faced fellow with a strong Afrikaans drawl.

Back in the Annex, Eirig lay on my bed. He had a pair of duplicate keys. 'My extra shift was cancelled.'

'And were you happy, dozing in this bed without its rightful occupant?'

'I breathed your aroma.'

I picked at a loose thread on my blouse.

In the yard behind the Annex, some youths were trying to light a fire in a dustbin. Perhaps being bonfire night, they thought no one would notice?

I slid up the sash-window 'Do you want some sweets?'

They looked bemused.

I threw out a box of fruit jellies, which the gang leader caught.

'Er ... thanks,' he stuttered.

I closed the window. 'Let's hope the bribe works.'

We played a game of Scrabble, then walked Dusty home.

On our return, we ran into Emma and her newly enamoured.

'Hey guys. You left before the fun started.'

'Oh?'

'First off, the student magazine's editor, when interviewing O'Rourke, took out her note-book and asked if it was in order to record their exchanges? The Master assented, but did not know that simultaneously someone else had switched on a voice recorder.'

'Cunning.'

'He threw out enough libellous opinions perhaps, to force the authorities to act.'

'That'll be no mean achievement ... against one of their own?'

Duncan said slowly, 'Then came the high-light of the evening. Some South African fellow stabbed that Russian diplomat – Alexei Ohotnikoff – two or three times in the groin.'

'Crikey. Was the Master embarrassed?'

'He fled ... unnoticed in the hubbub.'

In bed, I cuddled Eirig.

Gavin O'Rourke dreaded not rising to fame, when what he ought to dread was not finding his true self.

In the Song of Songs, Solomon's beloved says;

'I will go to the gate and draw the bolt,
Then embrace him for whom my soul longs.
Night after night on my bed,
I have sought him, my true love,
For his kisses are sweeter than wine.'

Eirig slept soundly and I fingered the scar on his skull and kissed it.

'My inclination to love you my sweet, is no *faux pas*, no wrong move.'

*   *   *   *

The corrected proofs for Matthew's book came and he ordered three hundred copies, whilst I sought out a book publicity agency which would place it on the standard websites, deal with book sales and set up the book's own website with a descriptive blurb, a couple of reviews, an 'About the author' section' and an 'How to order' box. Everything should be ready for the February launch.

On the second recto page, under 'Acknowledgements,' I alone figured in a slightly tongue-in-cheek accolade. The back cover bore Imogen's copy of the water-damaged picture from 1840. She had done a tidier job than had E. Flower.

The T-shirts were white with the book's title in red and the outline of the Hawthorn engine *North Shields* on it in green. The bookmarks had on them the book's title, barcode and website address. Two posters came to adorn the front of our table at Foyle's.

'Matthew, O'Rourke's switched to a Russian boyfriend ... well now a damaged Russian boyfriend.'

'Oh?'

'He's just been awarded the D.S.O.'

'The Distinguished Service Order?'

'No, the Dick Sliced Off.' I explained.

'Oh. You hear stories – usually set back in the fifties – of the K.G.B. infiltrating our educational establishments ... but not these days.'

'Perhaps their work is done?'

Next day, as nine of us threw netball balls back and forth to one another, it brought to my mind how at junior school – which always began with P.E. in the school-yard – we had thrown small bean-bags to one another.

Our main tactical strength was that since we did not know what we were doing, our opponents could never second guess our next move.

We had acquired a little more gymnastic agility and we all enjoyed a drink and a biscuit together at the bar afterwards in the Peppercorn Sports Centre.

We had now won one game, drawn one and lost seven.

I suggested that we should drink the Irn-Bru *before* the match, not after? I looked at Helena. 'Smile, do.'

She did so, reluctantly.

In a newsagent's, a crime magazine cover caught my eye. Djang Ming, a Birmingham jeweller, had been caught red-handed melting down cut-up fragments of a gold ingot with a blow-torch and a graphite crucible, then pouring the liquid into long thin moulds. Later they would be re-heated and put through a fine rolling mill to make wire and then used to make rings, the ends of short lengths being welded together and the result then buffed using emery or carborundum.

I imagined Laban Abrams doing the same in his cellar.

At the dress rehearsal the Pythian Prophetess had a lilac light shone on her, I a green one, like a pantomime villain. I wondered if a huge woolly spider might descend in the dark grey background?

Jolyon was visiting and he looked a little brighter. He had landed a job as a private tutor to two young boys, the sons of a deputy in the French *Assemblée Nationale*.

Simon, Imogen, Jolyon and I went into *The Old Lime Kiln* in Burford where we shared cheese and bacon baguettes and slurped orange or passion-fruit yoghurt drinks.

'Is your wound healing well ... I mean with no infection?'

'Yes. Mr Brownlee came to inspect it a couple of times.'

We sucked on our straws.

We touched on the power struggles going on behind the scenes at Newlove.

'Some wonder if Elaine-Marie wants to become Master?'

Simon recited one of Aesop's fables. 'Some frogs ask Zeus for a ruler, so he throws a log into their pond. After some initial trepidation, they sit on it and ask it if it is a god or an animal or what? It does not reply. Disappointed, they ask Zeus if they can have another ruler. Irritated, he sends them a water serpent, who gobbles them all up. The moral I suppose, is that there are worse things than idle or ineffective governors.'

I asked, 'If someone's political wishes came true, would it really bring them happiness?'

Simon thought about this. 'The exciting bit in any pursuit is the rough and tumble of getting there.'

Imogen added, 'If you're good-looking and courteous, you can get away with a bit of churlishness. If not, you have to be kinder and milder to compensate.'

'Poppy has a different view on this,' said Simon.

'Anyway,' Jolyon concluded, 'seriousness and hard work make the good moments good. It's like going to the gym I guess; tough but rewarding.'

We ordered shorts and some nuts.

*   *   *   *

Emma had taken to wearing a small platinum cross, hung on a fine chain round her throat and unsurprisingly this led to a visit from the boys in blue, who suggested that she now posed a threat to public order, an incitement to civil unrest.

I went with her to be interviewed by a police inspector.

'I don't think we should bow and scrape, but stick to our guns.'

'Still, we'll let them go first. See what slip-ups they make.'

Inspector Jayne Petty was a woman of around forty, thin-faced, off-puttingly pale-skinned, freckled and ginger-haired.

To one side sat a fellow of Middle-Eastern hue, with sunken cheeks, a white skull-cap and a large well-trimmed beard.

Petty looked at us dispassionately; someone with little or no emotion.

'May we see the complaint ... for triangulation?'

'That is only allowed if it is a level two investigation.'

'So does a complaint actually exist? No one's approached Emma about her cross.'

Emma drew her cross out from under her pullover. 'It is quite small. Did the complainant have a magnifying glass?'

'Or,' I appended, 'since it lives inside her cardigan, was he carrying an x-ray machine?'

This pin-prick of humour might – you would think – puncture her balloon ... but it did not.

'Those who saw it, saw it as a form of mockery. It has caused offence.'

'What if I dislike your tie?'

No reply

'If I felt I was wrong, I would say sorry,' said Emma, 'but I do not feel this is wrong ... that I need to wear a hair-shirt for it.'

Inspector Petty mostly avoided eye contact with us.

'Some reflection on your insensitivity – or provocation – would be appreciated,' she told her blotter. 'Emphasising your Anglo-Saxon and Christian backgrounds is culturally repugnant to many.'

By good fortune, my T-shirt was a white and green one with a large red dragon on it. I opened my jacket and pointed. 'Anglo-Saxon?'

'I don't understand.'

'She's Welsh,' Emma said heavily.

'If you think your job's bogus, why not resign?'

The unnamed fellow in the skull-cap harangued us softly, demanding respect for Islam. Someone in Sweden had recently and publicly burnt a copy of the Qur'an.

'This incident will be put on your record,' explained Petty and a second offence will lead to a hearing in a magistrates' court.'

The colourful flags we had drawn from under our tongues, had been to no avail.

'I have enough tasks to attend to,' Emma told her, 'without pandering to all this rubbish. We have only one life.'

'In the chapel where I go in Wales,' I persisted, 'we still believe in and revere the one true God, Father, Son and Holy Spirit and in a faith based on the Bible.'

Petty took a deep breath. 'You may very soon be forbidden from referring to such.'

EPILOGUE

On the final weekend of November, *The Eumenides* had its two performances, which happily went off well for such an obscure work. Impassioned cross-fires and odd pyrotechnic moments livened up the choruses and the reviews though sober, were appreciative of Carole's efforts to breathe life and humour into it ... perhaps as the ancient Athenians had done?

I cleared my room in the Annex and said goodbye to Alison, Emma and Libby.

Eirig and I visited our new farm, where the Sneddons were starting to pack up ready for their move back to Scotland.

'A local potato merchant who's hard up, has ten acres of good pasture for sale.'

We went to investigate, but it started to sleet, so we huddled in a log store and drank tea from our flasks.

We looked at the dry stone walls, the hedges and a covered feed trough.

'We'll start off quite modestly ... perhaps just twenty or thirty sheep ... not over-graze the fields ... learn how to look after our stock well.'

'What does that mean?'

'Or buy good hay if needs be? Did you read that chapter ... sweet-smelling and less than eighteen per cent moisture content?'

On Christmas Day Eirig was on duty so we celebrated Christmas in his signal box.

'Are there any trains on Christmas Day?'

'Three engineering ones.'

The stove was alight, glowing orange-white with coke ... and on it we heated up our Christmas dinners.

A small fall of snow – a little over an inch, hung silently on the trees.

'At our wedding? Is Ceinlys going to be a bridesmaid?'

'No, she'll let Megan stand in for her.'

It was so cosy and outside the snow increased; a quiescent and beautiful world.

And I do not know why, but I felt so happy.

THE END.